Sidhe Moved Through the Faire

Rie Sheridan Rose

DEDICATION
TO KAREN.
WHO BELIEVES IN ME.

Author's Note

Sidhe Moved Through the Faire takes its title from a traditional ballad, "She Moved Through the Fair." Sidhe (pronounced 'shee') literally means "people of the (fairy) hills." It is the Gaelic name for the fairies in both Ireland and the Highlands of Scotland. Usually these fairies are attracted to those who are beautiful as well as wealthy.

All names are Celtic in origin, so here's a pronunciation guide (*best guess):

NAME	PRONUNCIATION	MEANING	CHARACTER
Aisling	A sling	dream/vision	female Fae heroine
Ailill	AL yil	elf male	Fae hero
Caoimhe	KEE va	beauty/grace	human heroine
Fergal	FER ul	manly/valorous	human hero
Darragh	DAR row	oak	elder brother of twins
Eoghan	OH in	born of the yew	twins' father
Ailidh	*AL i	kind	twins' mother
Cian	KEE in	ancient	twins' uncle
Seamus	SHAY muss	derived from Jacob	Fergal's grandfather
Tadhg	TYG	poet	magistrate
Laoise	LEE sha	radiant girl	magistrate's wife
Rioghan	REE awn	little king	magistrate's son
Ruarc	ROO ark	hero/champion	tower guard captain
Sorcha	SUR a ka	bright/radiant	one of the hatchlings
Tanai	TAHN ee	slender/subtle	one of the hatchlings
Easnadh	AS na	musical sound	youngest hatchling

Further Definitions

(These are the traditional—I reserve the right to poetic license):

White Lady—all Celtic countries; goddess of death and destruction. Called the Dryad of Death and Queen of the Dead, this goddess was a Crone aspect of the Goddess.

The Dagda—Ireland; The Irish-Celtic god of the earth and treaties, and ruler over life and death. Dagda, or The Dagda, ("the good god") is one of the most prominent gods and the leader of the Tuatha Dé Danann. He is a master of magic, a fearsome warrior and a skilled artisan.

Morrigan—Ireland, Wales, Britain; a shape shifting war goddess of lust, magic, prophecy, revenge, war. Known as Great Queen, Supreme War Goddess, Queen of Phantoms, and Specter Queen. Variants: Morrigu, Morrighan, Morgan.

Seelie Court—The Court of the kind and benign fairy host, usually seen around twilight in long solemn processions. These fairies help the poor with gifts of corn and bread.

Unseelie Court—The evil counterpart of the Seelie Court is always unfavorable towards mankind. The Unseelie

Court ("Unholy Court") solely consists of those of the fairy-like beings that are the most ugly and evil.

Rhiannon—(Welsh, from Rigantona, Great Queen): white horse-queen-goddess

Avallach (British)—King of the Other Worldly kingdom of Avalon, an Orchard of Golden Apples of eternal life; father of Rhiannon.

Uaithne: The Dagda's Harp—The Dagda plays each of the seasons into being with his harp. The name of his harp, or in some legends, his harper, is Uaithne, which means pillar or post, but again it has a poetic meaning—internal rhyme.

The Wild Hunt—Stories of the Wild Hunt can be found in most of the legends of Northern Europe. From Norway to Orkney, there are many variations, but all of the versions have a great deal of similarity as well. All concern a faerie host that drive mortals unlucky enough to be their prey before horse and hound until they are caught and meet a disastrous end.

And now to the story...

CHAPTER ONE

"Shh...quiet! If they catch you, they'll pull your wings off and feed you to the witches!"

"Shut your gob, you git! They don't suffer witches. More like put us in cages and charge tuppance to see the beasties. But I'm no' afraid."

"You should be. Fae aren't welcome here."

"Mayhap they've never seen our like. Makes folk nervous. They'd learn better if the King would let us be seen."

"Still your tongue, fool!" Aisling glanced over her shoulder nervously, her iridescent wings trembling at the thought of what would happen to her lack wit of a brother if the King or one of his Court heard him talk so.

Ailill sniffed. "What's foolish is that we have to skulk around like shadows in our own country so as no' to be seen by the mortals. What's the harm in learning more about them? Can't we all just get along?"

Aisling shook her head vehemently, and hair the color of leaves in autumn cascaded about her shoulders. "They fear the Sidhe. Treat us like demons if they catch us about. We can't just walk up to them and say hello."

"And so we cower in the bushes," he muttered in disgust, sweeping a hand to take in the cavern-like space under the willow they crouched beneath. "'Tisn't fair."

"Maybe no', but it's safer."

"I want to go down there." Ailill pointed down the hill to the brightly colored market square. They could hear the din of lively trading going on even in their hidden bower half a league away. The smell of roasting meats and freshly baked bread wafted up to them on the breeze. "I can pretend to be one of them."

Aisling looked at her brother's winter-pale hair framing tilted green eyes. The tips of his ears peeked through the rough-cut thatch of hair, and his wings shimmered in the sunlight. "Only if they are blind." She rolled her own slanted eyes.

"All I have to do is pull in my wings and keep my ears covered. Come on, it would be an adventure. Doesn't it sound like fun to you?"

"It sounds like a damn fool thing to do, that's what it sounds like to me." She sniffed, and ran a grimy hand beneath her nose. "We shouldn't have come this close."

"I promise I'll take care of you, Aisling. Nothing bad will happen. Please...come with me." Ailill used the charming, wheedling tone that Aisling couldn't resist.

She hesitated. This was the most foolish thing he had asked for yet. To go down into the center of the human town and try and pretend to be a part of it...but on the other hand, the market was a siren call tugging at her heart. The sounds. The colors. The smells. It was all so...alive!

Life in the Sidhe Court could be so very dull. Especially for adolescent Fae with only a century or so under their wings. The twins weren't considered old enough to be part of the council, but they were considered too old to play with the hatchlings. Even Mother shooed them away in exasperation when they seemed more underfoot than needed. She had sent them out of the barrow today with orders to 'find something useful to do.'

After wandering for most of the morning, they had wound up here, crouched in the dirt beneath the willow. Ailill found humans fascinating. He had studied their ways since he was a tiny hatchling. Aisling usually went along because he was her brother. Her twin brother.

They were an uncommon pair. Twins were rare in the Sidhe society. If they had not been younger siblings of the house, things could have been worse, leading to complications over Father's council seat and other inheritance matters, but their elder brother Daragh held the place of heir in the unlikely event of Father's death.

Aisling glanced down the hill again, biting her lip nervously. She *did* want to go down there, if she was honest. But how could they hope to fit in?

She looked at her dress of spider gossamer and moonbeams and Ailill's tunic of autumn leaves over moleskin breeches. They looked about as human as the King's prize stag.

Ailill caught her glance. "Don't worry. I have a plan. See there?" He pointed to an isolated cottage on the other side of the hill.

Aisling followed the direction of his finger and saw laundry spread to dry on the bushes beside the cottage. "What are you thinking, Ailill?"

"I'm saying we steal us some clothes—loose ones to fit on over these—and we go to the Faire." He grinned at her.

"What about our wings?"

"I can pull on a smock over mine. I've done it before."

She glanced at him sharply. "When?"

A faint tinge of color bloomed on his pale cheeks. "Never you mind. I'll find you a table cover or bit of bed linen you can drape into a bodice, and you can pull your wings down around your shoulders like a shawl of your own."

Aisling sighed. He obviously had given the matter a great deal of thought, and he was usually right about such things. It *could* be very exciting...

"Oh, all right," she murmured. "Let's go to the Faire."

They slid down the hill and ran like deer to the lea of the cottage with the drying laundry. Ailill took charge, grabbing several garments off the bushes and then herding her toward a nearby copse of trees.

Safely out of sight once more, he handed her a heavy serge skirt and a length of coarse linen. "Put these on."

"Do I have to? Can't I just wear the skirt?"

He eyed her critically. "I suppose...if you pull your wings down tight. Slip the tips into the waist."

She pulled on the skirt and adjusted her wings, surprised to find there was no discomfort. In fact, the soothing warmth of her wings against her bare arms felt wonderfully comforting.

Ailill hurriedly drew on a pair of rough breeches and slipped a loose smock over his head. Sweeping his hair back and over his ears, he looked like a farm lad wearing his father's castoffs.

"Cover your ears, Aisling. They stick up to the sky."

"Well, how do you propose I cover them? I haven't a kerchief."

"Use that bit of linen," he ordered. "It will make do."

She wound it about her head, making sure the points of her ears were well concealed. "How do I look?"

"Except for the fact your eyes look like an emerald cat's, you'll do." He shrugged. "Let's go to the Faire," Ailill said with a grin, catching her hand.

Hand in hand, they wandered to the square. Aisling kept glancing about nervously, sure they would be caught at any moment and dragged away to be locked into a cage somewhere. All the wicked stories she had heard about humans reverberated in her head.

When someone brushed her arm, she shrieked and jumped behind Ailill.

"I beg your pardon, lass," said the old man who had accidentally touched her.

"She's a bit daft," replied Ailill, with a condescending pat on her arm. "She's afeard everyone is boggles and beasties. Can't rightly take her out of the house without she starts like a skittish colt at every passing breeze."

Aisling bristled under the description. "'Tisn't so! Why, I've seen you—"

The old man smiled, his eyes sparkling with fun. "Ah, 'tis kinfolk you are, not sweethearts."

Aisling felt her cheeks grow hot. "I don't have a sweetheart," she murmured.

The old man's eyes darkened as the pupils widened. "Ah, but you shall, lass," he answered. He turned to Ailill, "And you as well, lad. But mark you both well, there are some things best left unseen and others left unsaid. Be ware your hearts, lest you leave them at the Faire."

Ailill made a rude noise. "Seems I was wrong, old man. *You* are the daft one. We are merely traveling through and saw the market bustling. We thought to take an hour's rest and maybe shop for a betrothal gift for my sister here. She is to be married come harvest."

The old man nodded sagely. "It may be as you say, or..." He leaned in close, whispering words scented with onion, "...it may be you Fae folk decided to play with the mortal realm for a wee bit of sport."

Aisling clapped her hand to her mouth to stifle a squeak of terror. He knew who, or worse, *what* they were.

"Don't worry, lass," he said with a smile, reaching out to pat her arm reassuringly. "I'll no' tell anyone, and your disguise will fool the simple folk. Those of us born with a caul can see the Sidhe for what they be, no matter what the disguise. And we see other things as well. I spoke truly now. Have a care for your heart, lest it be broken."

She nodded, wide-eyed. "I swear we mean no harm, sir. If it be best, we'll go at once."

"Nay, lass. Enjoy the morning. 'Tis a beautiful one, and the market is always lively on Faire day." He reached out and took her hand, pressing something into it. "Use this to advantage. It will aid your disguise." With a little bow, he scurried away into the crowd.

Aisling looked down at her hand. There were two shining gold crowns in the palm of it. She gasped, and Ailill grabbed the coins from her.

"That's mine!" she protested, trying to snatch them back.

"We share, as always," he retorted then sighed reluctantly. "But if it will make you feel better..." He grudgingly slapped one of the heavy coins back into her hand. "There. One for each. But spend it slow. It's all we got."

Aisling felt the weight of the coin in her hand. It was solid and substantial and somehow made the day feel more surreal. The Fae needed no money. What they wanted from each other was freely given, and property belonged to the King. No one wanted for sustenance, and material possessions were limited to clothes and kit.

"I don't know what to do with this," she confided.

Ailill rolled his eyes. "You are such a ninny. If you find something you like, give it to the merchant, and you'll get what you want. Even a hatchling knows that."

Aisling sniffed. "I suppose you traffic in gold all the time, with your worldly ways."

He had the courtesy to blush. "No, but I've heard stories. And so would you, if you kept your ears open more."

Aisling looked at her brother's discomfort with a fond smile. There was no need to tease him. He did know more than she, and she relied upon him to do so. Ailill was the adventuresome one. He was the one who found the robins' nests and the rose hips. She was the one who wove the moonbeams and mended his clothes when he fell from the trees. Together they were stronger than apart.

"You are right, as usual. Come." She held out her hand. "Let's go back to exploring."

He grinned and took the outstretched hand. "Aye. That meat smells devilish good. I intend to eat myself silly."

"Won't be far to go," she teased.

Ailill laughed aloud.

The Fae twins started forward through the crowded paths. Booths of bright canvas were lined on either side of the narrow walkways, and they often had to shove their way through when customers bargained on both sides of the path at once.

Aisling feared for her wings. They would be so easily crushed in this madness. She kept tugging nervously at the tips to make sure they were firmly in her waistband. Casting an envious eye at the slightly humped appearance Ailill got from having his covered, she wished she had a shift of her own to pull over them.

They arrived at last at the meat-pie booth, and Ailill bought two of the steaming pasties, handing her one with a flourish. "Here. You look half-starved."

He took his change from the vendor and stood glancing from the coins to his pie. "This is a nuisance," he growled. "How do they deal with carrying so much?"

"Stick your coins in your pouch and move along, lad. You're keeping the customers away," ordered the pie seller.

Startled, the twins moved out of the path to a spot between two booths where a square of trampled grass suggested someone had pulled up stakes early. They sat upon the crushed grass to eat their prizes.

"We need something to carry this in," mumbled Ailill around a mouthful of pasty, shoving out the fistful of small coins.

"Perhaps I can help you there," murmured a deep voice behind them.

Chapterr Two

Aisling squeaked, almost choking on a mouthful of pie.

Ailill closed his fist tight around the coins. "What you want?" he growled, leaping to his feet and standing guard over his sister.

The newcomer laughed, holding up his hands in a gesture of placation. "I meant no harm, sir. I merely sell pouches at the booth across the way. I happened to be passing and heard your comment."

Aisling looked up at the man from her position on the ground. He seemed to tower to the sky. His hair was black as midnight, and his eyes were the blue of the summer sky. She stared up at him in awe. He was the most beautiful being she had ever seen. Suddenly, she felt a sharp kick to her thigh.

"Close your mouth, you git. You look like a simpleton with your jaw gaping and a mouthful of food."

Mortified, Aisling hid her face in her hands. She wanted to melt through the ground like the morning frost.

"Fear no', my Lady," came a gentle voice. A warm hand was placed upon her shoulder. "A gentleman sees only what a lady wishes him to see." The obvious rebuke in the man's words thrilled her heart.

Finally someone who would put Ailill in his place. She loved her brother, but he could be a royal nuisance.

She peeked out from between her fingers to find their new acquaintance hunkered down beside her. Up close, he was even more beautiful—or handsome as the mortals would quibble, saying "beautiful" was too feminine. "Thank you, my Lord," she whispered, her voice a mere thread of sound.

He smiled, and Aisling felt as if the sun had risen directly in front of her.

Stretching out a hand, he rose to his feet. "Come, my Lady. You shouldn't sit here on the cold ground. I have a place in my shop where you may sit and eat at your leisure."

It was only then Aisling realized she still clutched her mangled meat pie in one grimy fist. She flung it to the ground, earning a squawk of protest from Ailill. She ignored him. "'Tis no matter, my Lord. I-I have finished."

"Well, come and rest awhile anyway. My booth is warm, and there is a chill in the air. I wouldn't want you to catch your death, Lady...?" His voice trailed off, the question unspoken between them.

"Aisling," she whispered. "My name is Aisling."

There was a strangled sound from the direction of her twin, but she didn't care. She knew the danger of telling a stranger her true name, but her whole heart trusted this man she had met only moments before.

"Fergal O'Connor, at your service," he said, with a flourishing bow. He offered her his arm, and she took it shyly.

The feel of the muscles beneath his shirt thrilled her in a way she'd never felt before. He was so big, and warm, and *real*. He made her entire being tingle.

Ailill snorted behind her. "Daft as a March hare you are! Well, I'll no' stand for it." He grabbed for her arm. "Come away, Aisling. 'Tis time we were for home."

"'Twas your idea to come," she sniffed. "I'll no' be toted home like a baby. I am free to go where I choose, am I not?"

"You can go to the devil for all I care!" He started to stamp away from them and then turned abruptly. "I'll no' be responsible for your trouble, Aisling. You're on your own from here on out."

"I can take care of myself, Ai—" She stopped, biting her lip. No, she would not give his name so freely. Her own was hers to give or hold, but Ailill's belonged to him, and he did not trust the mortal. She bowed her head.

"She will be safe with me, Lord," Fergal offered softly. "I shall see she comes to no harm."

Ailill's eyes were hard chips of emerald. "'Tis all one with me. If she wishes to play the fool, I've done with her. But I'll no' suffer the consequences." He turned on his heel and stalked away.

Aisling watched him go through a mist of tears. They were twins—closer than blood—and he was abandoning her. Which of them was the fool?

⁂

Blind temper made him leave her. Ailill realized that as soon as he had walked far enough to settle down. But sheer stubbornness prevented him from going back.

He scowled down at the path, too angry to watch where he was going. Sometimes she was such an innocent. Trusting a mortal, and *she*—who had been too petrified to want to come to town in the first place. He'd let her stew in her own juices until she realized how wrong she'd been, and then—

There was a sharp cry of dismay, and he found himself on his backside in the center of the path. Sitting in front of him, surrounded by broken eggshells and dusty yolks was the most beautiful creature *he* had ever seen.

An expression of woe darkened storm-gray eyes as she surveyed the wreckage of her upturned basket. Wisps of harvest-gold hair had fallen loose from the intricate pile atop her head, and her cheeks were scarlet with mortification. As he watched, a tear broke free of her control and slipped down her smooth cheek to trickle from her button nose.

His heart was gone.

"Oh, what shall I do?" wailed his angel. "That was the whole day's gathering, and Mam waiting at home for the egg money. We were to eat for a week on those coins!"

He reached forward and pressed his whole handful of change into her palm. "It was my fault entirely. If this will no' do, let me know. I will find more."

She looked down at the coins in her hand. "'Tis more than generous, my Lord...but I cannot take it." She tried to give the money back. "'Twas no more than my own fault for day-dreaming."

He closed her fingers about the coins. "No, 'twas mine." He smiled. "I'll convince you of that if I have to—but perhaps no' in the middle of the road."

Rising lithely to his feet, he held down a hand to her. "May I escort you to where you are going, my Lady?"

"Oh..." She took his outstretched hand, and let him pull her up. "Caoimhe Sinclair. 'Tis home I'll be returning to now, my Lord." She gestured helplessly at the slime-trails of egg soaking into the dusty road by way of explanation.

He shook his head in bemusement. Perhaps it was the way of women to trust strangers so with their very souls. And yet, something in him responded to the trust. "They call me Ailill," he answered, conscious of how unfinished the name would sound to a mortal.

Her eyes widened. "Are you for knowing what your name means?"

His smile broadened. "Aye. Though some would argue the appropriateness of it, saying I be more demon than elf." He thought back to Aisling's reaction to Fergal and realized perhaps she wasn't so daft after all.

"Now, I'll ask you again, my Lady Caoimhe. May I escort you home?"

"'Tis quite a ways outside of town, my Lord. I am sure you have better things to do on Faire day." There was a wistfulness in her voice, and her gray glance roamed the nearby stalls.

"May I escort you around the Faire then?"

She blushed prettily and dropped him a bobbed curtsey. "It would be my pleasure, sir."

He tucked her arm firmly through his elbow, as he had seen Fergal do with Aisling's, and they began to stroll through the Faire.

Everywhere the sights and sounds of market day assaulted the senses. The brightly colored canvas of the tents snapped in the breeze, and the cries of stall owners hawking their wares rose in the air. "Fine laces!

No better to be found!" "Knives sharpened—guaranteed to please." "Small beer and ale. Quench your thirst here!" And the smells...fresh bread warring with the aroma of a nearby corral, rare spices perfuming the air from a silken tent.

Ailill didn't know where to look. The sheer volume of information overwhelmed his senses. He fingered a bit of silk, marveling at its slippery coolness. It was like trying to hold a moonbeam. Aisling would love something like this.

He frowned. There was no call to be so hard on her...she'd been so sheltered, after all. How could she be expected to know the ways of the mortal world?

A soft voice interrupted his thoughts. "It displeases you, Lord Ailill?"

"What?" He started out of his reverie and then realized how it must look. "No—'tis a fine bit of cloth. I was thinking of something else. And I'm no lord, child. Just Ailill."

Caoimhe laughed. "And I'm no child, lo—Ailill. I am one and twenty, and fast and away to becoming an old maid."

"Someone as beautiful as you? Are the mortals of this realm quite mad?"

"Mortals?"

Ailill wanted to bite his wayward tongue off at the roots. "Aye...for one as beautiful as you must be from the land of Faerie."

She blushed prettily, the rose flushing up her neck and into her lovely cheeks. "You mock me, Lord."

"No! 'Twas no' my intent. I swear it."

"Then you must think me a bloody fool," she continued,

her voice no longer gentle but hard and bitter. "The Fae do no' truck with mortals, and if they did, 'twould no' be with a common farmer's daughter such as me."

Ailill felt tightness in his chest as he contemplated his next words. The mere thought of the proposal he wished to make set his blood pounding in his eyes. Not here. He could not do it here.

Reaching out, he grabbed her hand. "Come with me," he ordered urgently, pulling her along after him.

"W-where are we going?" There was an edge of fear to her voice.

He hated himself for frightening her, but he had to get her away from the market crowds where they could talk more privately. "You'll see."

She stumbled and nearly fell. "I-I cannot go so fast. Please!"

He stopped and looked at her. "Do you trust me?"

Her eyes studied his face. "Aye," she answered softly. "Lord help me, I do."

"Then you must come with me without question, and I will tell you all in due time."

Caoimhe's shoulders straightened, and he could see the resolve shoring her up. "I will come with you. But I cannot go so fast."

"There's a willow at the top of yonder hill—" He pointed to the hidey-hole. "When we get there, I'll tell you everything."

"All right," she murmured. "Can we stop a moment at the bottom of the hill so I can leave off the egg money?"

His heart jumped. The only cottage near the bottom of the hill was the one where they had stolen their clothes this morning.

"I recognized Da's smock the moment I saw you," she continued calmly. "I mended it just there..." She laid a small hand on his breastbone, where a tiny triangular tear had been neatly sewn. "But we will no' miss the clothes. Though I do wonder what a fine young man such as yourself needed with my best skirt." She smiled up at him, a dimple peeking from her cheek.

"'Twas for my sister," he blurted out.

"No' a sweetheart?"

"Nay."

"Then, 'tis all well. May she have good use of it. Shall we go?"

They continued along their way at a slower pace, but more at ease with each other. Caoimhe pointed out the sights of the village as they walked.

When they passed the spot where he and Aisling had parted company, Ailill hesitated. He should tell her...something. But he could think of nothing to say. He would see her when she wandered home and apologize for his rude behavior then. They were both having something of an adventure today.

He waited outside while Caoimhe took the money inside the cottage. The sun was well past noon now, and he wanted to be home before dark.

She came back out of the cottage without her basket, a shawl draped about her shoulders. "I am ready," she said quietly, reaching out for his hand.

He led her up the hill and into the willow bower. When they were hidden from mortal eyes, he dropped her hand and put both of his upon her shoulders.

"Do you trust me, Caoimhe Sinclair?"

"With my life," she breathed.

"Will you follow me now?"
"To the ends of the earth."
"To the land of the Sidhe?"

CHAPTER THREE

The inside of Fergal's booth was indeed warm and dry. Aisling glanced around the structure curiously. She was used to the barrow, where the walls were of earth and stone. She could not understand why anyone would cut down trees to build something so impermanent. A tree was a gift to the world and could shelter many beings for decades. A flimsy bower like this would blow down in a good strong wind or fall in seconds to flame.

But Fergal was obviously proud of his shop, and she could understand why, despite her reservations. His goods were of the finest leather, soft and supple to the touch or well-cured and sturdy, depending on the projected use. His pouches were decorated with hand-tooled designs, and one with a pattern of leaves caught her attention. She touched the soft green leather with one fingertip.

"Do you like it?" he asked her eagerly.

"Oh, yes. 'Tis beautiful."

"Then you must have it. Here." He picked up the pouch and started toward her—then saw she had no belt to attach it to. "You need this as well," he murmured, lifting a darkly tanned belt worked with an ivy pattern. He threaded the belt through the loop of the pouch and then hesitated. "May I?" he asked, gesturing to her slender waist.

Aisling felt the color rise in her cheeks. "Aye," she murmured shyly, lifting her arms out of the way.

He reached around her and brought the belt together in the front, cinching it tight around her waist.

Aisling gasped as a sharp pain flared from the tips of her wings to her shoulders. She had forgotten they were tucked into the band of her skirt, and the belt was pinching them cruelly.

Fergal stepped back, his face a picture of distress. "Did I hurt you, lady?"

"'Tis nothing," she hastened to reassure him, surreptitiously easing the belt away from her wings. "A brief spasm merely. I suffer them now and again."

"Come and sit down," he commanded, so gently she could not take offense. He took her elbow and led her to a tall stool beside the shop counter.

Aisling perched upon the stool. Its height brought her eyes level with Fergal's, and she took advantage of the opportunity to study him further. His thick, black hair waved back from his forehead, save for one errant curl that brushed its expanse. The lashes shielding his blue eyes were so thick they made them appear darker. His mouth was generous and quirked in an easy grin. He was strongly built, with a dancer's grace. She found her thoughts straying places where they should not go and reined them in sharply. She had best be ware. It would be easy to forget who and what she was in the presence of a man like this one.

* * *

Fergal O'Connor found it hard to concentrate on being a gentleman in the presence of the mysterious beauty who had materialized in his life. Aisling, was she? True and she lived up to the name. She was a dream indeed...a vision driving him to distraction, with hair the color of Yule flame and eyes as green as the sea. There was something ethereal about her—waiflike. He wanted to protect her. Shelter her from the world and its cruelties...and he hardly knew her.

She was looking at him now with those big green eyes, tilted at the corners like a cat's. Something was distressing her...she had the edge of her lip caught between her teeth as if sealing in words that wanted to escape.

"Is there something wrong, lady?"

"I—no...no, I can't tell. I mustn't."

"Whatever secret you have is safe with me."

"If only I could be sure of that," she sighed, her voice a whisper.

"I swear on my life—"

"No!" She jumped off the stool in alarm, laying a hand across his lips. "No...you mustn't say such. Promise me!"

He nodded. The day was becoming odder by the moment.

She stepped away, her back to him. Suddenly, her shoulders straightened, as if some resolve had shored her up. She turned toward him.

"Can I tell you? Will you keep my secret?"

"Aye, lady. For as long as you say."

She took a deep breath, and then her hands fumbled at the waist of her skirt. Something moved in the muted sunlight from the front of the shop, and he gasped. What he had taken to be a gossamer shawl draped about her shoulders unfolded into a pair of translucent wings, which caught and reflected the light like sunlit rainbows. They were as insubstantial as spider webs and looked heartbreakingly fragile.

Instinctively, his hand moved in the sign against the evil eye, and her hopeful expression dissolved. Tears filled those lovely eyes, threatening to spill over onto cheeks pale as alabaster. The lovely wings drooped of their own accord, and Aisling retreated into the far corner of the shop. She curled into a little ball upon the floor, hiding her face in her hands. Sobs began to shake her shoulders, and her wings curved about her protectively.

"Curse me for a fool!" Fergal exclaimed, hurrying across the room. He knelt before her, reaching out to lay a hand on her shoulder. "Aisling, I did no' mean..."

She cried harder.

He could think of no words to make a difference, so he simply gathered her into his arms, taking care not to crush the fragile wings. His lips brushed the top of her head, as if offering comfort to a child. "There, there, lambling. I will keep your secret. You are safe with me. I swear it."

What was he to do? He had lost his heart to a Fae...

* * *

Caoimhe Sinclair stared at the man in front of her. Had he just said...? "What are you asking me, Ailill?"

"Did I no' make myself plain? I want for you to come with me to Faerie."

"Are you daft?"

He dropped his hands from her shoulders. "So, you

29

think 'tis mad I am? Shall I prove to you different?" He jerked the smock over his head, and his wings sprang free, trembling from the sudden release.

Caoimhe's hand flew to her mouth. It was true. He was Sidhe!

"'Tis no' the end of the world, lass. I do no' eat babies for dinner or curse the cows for lack of respect."

Her mind reeled. The stories...

He must have seen her thoughts in her face, for he continued, "Make no mistake, not all Sidhe are so inclined. There are two courts among the Fae, one for good and one for ill. 'Tis the Unseelie beasties that give all Fae our ill-name. We are peaceful folk in the Seelie Court and only want to live unfettered and unafraid. Can you say you want any different?"

She shook her head slowly. "Nay. 'Tis what everyone wants...but I thought the Fae beyond our needs and wishes."

"Sure and we've got to live, same as you," he said with a laugh. "There is much in common between us."

She stared at his wings, trembling slightly still, and reached a tentative hand forward. "May I—?"

"Touch them? Sure and they won't dissolve, for all they look like spun sugar."

He moved closer, and she touched the delicate membrane. It was warm and vibrated beneath her fingertip. "Can you fly?"

"If the wind is right, for short distances. They are more for show than use. Once we could flit about the countryside like hummingbirds, but we've gotten bigger, and our wings have no'. I've heard it whispered they may disappear entirely in time..."

"Would you be sorry to see them go?"

"'Twon't be in my time, but aye. I would. Our wings say we are Sidhe!" He sprang into the air, and hovered there, his wings beating. The light reflected off of their iridescent panels like sunlight on water.

The sight dazzled her eyes. "How beautiful," she whispered.

His bare feet touched down with a slight stumble. He rested his hands on his knees and breathed deeply, chest heaving. "'Tis hard work, flying."

She made up her mind. "I will go with you if you still want me."

"Are you sure?" he asked eagerly. "There is so much I want to show you."

"I am sure. There is little for me here, and no one much to miss me. I want to see your Faerie."

* * *

Aisling sobbed as if her heart would break. She had hoped he would see past her differences to the soul of her, but he was a mortal man and could bear no truck with Fae. She had seen it in his gesture and the look of shock on his face when he saw her wings unfurl.

And then she felt his arms around her and the whispered words of comfort. She felt his lips upon her hair and turned a startled face upward in perfect time to catch his lips on hers. A surge of heat ran through her at the touch, and she felt as if she stood on top of ground just lightning struck.

"Oh!" she cried, pulling back in his arms.

"I'm sorry," Fergal murmured, dropping his arms

to his sides and rocking back on his heels. "I did no' mean to take advantage."

"No, it's just...I've never...what were you doing?"

"You mean the kiss, lass? You've never been kissed?"

"Nay. 'Tis no' something we do amongst the Fae. What is it for?"

Fergal looked taken aback. "What do you mean 'for'? It is a way to soothe someone in pain, to show affection, to—" Unaccountably, he blushed scarlet.

Aisling cocked her head quizzically. "To what?"

"To tell someone how much you care for them."

"Isn't that the same as show affection?"

"Nay, lass. I mean to...dash it all! It is a way to say 'I love you' without the words."

"And how did you mean it?" she asked gravely, her heart beating madly in her chest.

"I-I don't know. I thought I was merely offering comfort...but now, I'm no' so sure."

"Would you teach me more of this...kissing?" she asked shyly.

He bent his dark head, and his lips pressed firmly onto hers. They were warm and velvet soft.

She felt again the same dizzying sensation of standing too close to a lightning strike and moaned softly in her throat. Then she felt his lips move against her own, and a gentle touch against her closed mouth, nudging her lips to part. She complied and felt his tongue slip inside her mouth. It was all she could do to keep from laughing. It felt silly...and yet, it was most satisfying.

She let her arms come up to curve around his neck and felt his own gently encircle her waist once more, taking care for her wings. The kiss deepened, and she felt herself melting into him. She would drown in the sensations...

Abruptly, he broke contact, leaning back on his haunches.

Aisling bowed her head in misery. "I did no' do it correctly?" she asked softly.

"No, child—far from it. You did it all too well." His voice was hoarse and his breathing rapid.

"I am no child," she retorted. "I am past one hundred years...even if the King thinks we are no more than striplings."

His eyes widened. "One hundred?"

"Aye. How old did you think me?"

"You look no more than ten and seven. I thought myself ancient compared to one as young as you."

"Does it make a difference? How old are you?"

"I am five and twenty and long past the age to marry. I have been searching all my life for the woman of my dreams—and she is a Fae." He shook his head with a rueful chuckle. "My grand-da told me my life would be complicated."

"What did he say?"

"He said I would meet my heart's desire and lose everything in the getting of her. That I would come to know terrible sorrow and win through to great joy. But I do no' truck too deeply with the mumblings of an old man—for all he wears the caul."

Aisling started. "Is your grandfather white of hair and deep of voice? Does he walk with a slight limp to his gait?"

"Aye. You talk as if you know him."

"I believe I met him this morning...he told me to be ware, lest I lose my heart and find it broken."

"It sounds like the old man. Do you credit his prophecy?"

"I do no' know," she whispered. "But I do believe I've lost my heart..."

CHAPTER FOUR

Ailill had shed the rest of his borrowed clothes, and he and Caoimhe stood before the barrow shielding the entrance to Faerie. "I will keep you safe, Caoimhe. Trust me."

"If I didn't, I wouldn't have come." She smiled, but he saw the tension behind her brave facade.

He dropped a swift kiss on her forehead—Ailill was not as sheltered as his sister and no stranger to the art of kissing. "That's my girl," he murmured. To be honest, he was being less than truthful with the lass. He was not at all sure what reception he would get when he brought a human through the magic gate. There was something deep inside him though, demanding he try.

"Close your eyes," he told her.

She did as she was bid without question.

Ailill turned to the stone doorway and moved his hands in the complicated pattern that opened the magic portal. The stone grated back along its track with a rumble of protest, almost as if the rock itself were warning him against his course.

Ailill shook off the fancy and took Caoimhe's hand in his. "Do no' open your eyes until I give you leave. It is for your own safety."

"As you say," she agreed, nodding her head. "I trust you, Ailill."

"Good girl." He stepped through the portal, leading his precious charge forward and into the land of the Fae. The path was smooth and straight, wending its way through the enchanted kingdom with no risk of falling. But, though the path was safe, he could feel Caoimhe tremble and guessed the cause. It could not be easy to go blind into territory so strange.

Once they had passed beyond sight of the door, Ailill stopped and raised a hand to Caoimhe's cheek. "You can open your eyes now."

Those beautiful gray eyes fluttered open, and she looked around her in wonder. "Oh, Ailill...it's spectacular."

He looked around him, seeing his homeland through her eyes. It *was* spectacular. Delicately branched trees raised their limbs to the azure sky. The leaves were shades of green and gold and sparkled like gemstones in the sunlight. A babbling brook ran nearby, chuckling to itself as it wound its way through the emerald grass.

The crystalline clarity of the air made the atmosphere on the other side of the door seem heavy and blurred.

In the mortal realm, smoke from the cook fires and smithy hazed the sky even on the clearest morning. In the land of the Fae, where magic banished need for fires, there was no such distortion, and from the top of a rise, they could see three leagues in any direction. Gently rolling hills spread out around them like the swell of the sea, and in the far distance hung the spires of the King's castle like carved diamonds reflecting the sunlight.

Hearing the sound of pounding hooves nearby, Ailill pulled Caoimhe into the shadow of a tree, a finger to his lips signaling her to remain quiet. A unicorn broke from the trees, tossing its magnificent head, horn glittering in the sunlight. It gave a high, musical whinny, and its mare trotted up to it, touching her horn to his, tip to tip. Finally, a colt, still stiff-legged in its gait, its horn a mere nub beneath its forelock, ran up to nuzzle against its mother. The family stood like a statue frozen in time for a dozen heartbeats then broke and cantered off into the distance.

Caoimhe let her breath out in a shuddering sigh. "Oh! I never thought I'd see such magic."

"There is more for me to be showing you, girl," replied Ailill. He brushed a stray golden tendril back behind her ear. "This is a place of wonders...but there is no wonder here I would no' trade for the sight of you."

Her cheeks bloomed crimson, and she dropped her gaze. "You jest with me."

"Nay! I mean every word of it. I would give you all of Faerie, were it mine to give, and never look back."

Her eyes darkened, and their expression grew troubled. "You don't know anything about me, Ailill."

"I know enough. I know you are pure of heart, or you would no have seen the unis. They cannot be seen by the wicked. I know you are brave of spirit, or you would no' have trusted me and come hither blind. I know you are the most beautiful creature I have ever laid my eyes upon in a century of searching."

Caoimhe pulled free of him, turning her back and walking away. "I-I don't know what to say to you, Ailill. This is happening so fast my head is spinning. I am merely a farmer's daughter, used to milking cows and harvesting eggs. You are something out of a dream. Perhaps I should no' have come."

"I am so very pleased you did..." he replied shyly. "I am often chided for my foolishness, but I am serious as the lightning when I say I would gladly spend the rest of my days proving it to you."

She turned toward him, her gray eyes magnified by the tears standing in their depths. "The Fae are such fickle creatures. Their attention wanders with the wind. If I gave you my heart, how long would it be before it was given me back again in a thousand pieces?"

"Is there no way I can prove to you what I say?"

"I know not. I cannot lie to you and give some easy answer. Mayhap, in time, I will believe."

He caught up her hand and pressed it to his heart. "Then I will hasten that day in every way I can. But for now, I will show you more of Faerie. You will come to love it so, I'm certain you will be content to stay with me and be my love."

Her mouth worked, as if striving to suppress a smile at his exuberance, but she finally gave in, and her delighted laugh rang out. "If any can work such a spell on such as I, it would be you, Ailill of the Sidhe."

He slipped his arm around her waist, and she allowed her head to rest upon his shoulder. Tentatively, her arm slipped beneath his wings to encircle his slim waist. They walked on, entwined like lovers, under the perfect sky.

The crystalline air made distances deceptive, and the spires of the castle hung ever before them at the horizon, growing no nearer. After an hour or more of walking, Caoimhe cried out and crumpled to the ground.

Ailill knelt beside her, his heart in his throat. "What is it? What's wrong?"

She winced, and slipped her dainty shoe off her foot. "There's a pebble in my shoe," she replied. "These slippers were no' meant for travel." With a rueful smile, she held up the shoe for him to see. The thin sole was worn clear through. "I meant to change them after Faire, but 'twas my vanity to look my best at market. When we stopped at the cottage, I could no' take the time, for my Mam would have questioned my intentions."

Ailill sank down beside her, his legs crossed under him. "You should have said something, lass. I've been pushing you hard to get to the city before nightfall. I don't have the same problem myself, you see—" He held up one bare foot, hard as horn from a lifetime unshod. "—we don't truck with such." He grinned. "We'll rest for a bit then. There's a brook over this hill, can you make it that far?"

"I think so."

He helped her to her feet and half-carried her to the bank of the little stream. Borrowing her kerchief, he dipped it in the cool water and bathed her foot. There was a small stone bruise rising on her heel, and he rested a hand against it for a moment.

She gasped and studied his face. "The pain is gone." She glanced down at her foot. The bruise was gone as well. "How did you do that?"

He winked at her. "'Tis a Faerie secret. Are you hungry?"

"Aye. A mite."

He rose to his feet and leapt into the air, flying up to the branches of the tree they rested beneath. He quickly picked a handful of ripe *driw* fruit, the sweet purple globes heavy with juice.

Landing lightly beside her, he handed Caoimhe two of the rich fruit and then sank to the ground. "Be careful," he cautioned. "The juice will stain cloth, though it will wash off the skin."

He took a bite of his fruit, savoring the thick, sweet juice.

Caoimhe laughed. "'Tis good it will no stick to flesh because you wear a purple beard, my Lord."

"'Tis the only sort I'll ever wear," he retorted with a smile. "We do no' grow beards in Faerie. Though 'tis said—" He broke off abruptly. No, he did not wish to speak of that.

"'Tis said what, my Lord?"

"Never mind. Eat up, Lady. We have long to go before dark, and the sun is falling to the east."

"To the west, you mean?"

"Nay, Lady. The sun does set in the east in Faerie. All is widdershins to the land beyond the barrow."

He saw her shiver. "Do no' fear, Caoimhe. I will no let anything harm you."

She smiled up at him, her face a trifle pale. "No' of your choosing, Ailill...but it is all so strange."

"Have you finished your fruit?"

She took a last bite of the fruit she had been eating, and thrust the second into the pocket of her apron. "What should I do with this?" she asked, holding up the pit of the fruit, to which some pulp still clung.

"I'll take care of it." He took the *driw* stone from her hand and held it up above his head, whistling sharply between his teeth.

A large white bird sailed down to snatch the seed from his hand then curved away toward the top of the next hill. It landed and scratched at the ground, for all the world as if digging a pit. It dropped the seed neatly into the hole and smoothed the ground over it, first with talons and then with wingtip before soaring back into the heavens.

"What was *that*?" she cried in amazement.

"Twas a *yautha* bird," explained Ailill, dusting his hands together. "They are the guardians of the trees. They protect the saplings and plant the seedlings. Legend has it they are the souls of those who chose to die rather than live eternal. When they have served a thousand days they return to dust forever."

"Oh, how sad..."

"In a way, I suppose. But 'tis their choice, and who am I to gainsay it?" He shrugged. "Shall we go forward?"

She rose to her feet, kicking off her other shoe as she did so. "When in Faerie, do as the Fae," she murmured with a dimpled grin.

He took her hand, and they wandered on. As they walked, Ailill pointed out the wonders of his homeland—a stately gryphon flying across a meadow; a natural fountain bubbling up through a gemstone encrusted basin; waving fields of *lothali* flowers with their crimson blossoms on slender golden stalks.

Caoimhe delighted in all she saw, her excited exclamations lifting his heart skyward. "Oh, Ailill! It is all so beautiful."

He felt a momentary pang of conscience disturb his happiness. No, it was not *all* beautiful... He cast an uneasy eye toward the eastering sun. They needed to be under shelter before nightfall. It was not safe for the Seelie Court to wander the hills at night. At night, the land belonged to the dark. And the Unseelie Court held sway.

It would be more than their lives were worth to be caught by the Unseelie masses. A human in the land of the Fae? That alone would be death to his beloved. How had it gotten so late so quickly? Would they make the aerie before dark, or should he begin to seek some shelter?

Finally, he could see the castle and its surrounding dwellings over the rise of the next hill. The disk of the sun was touching the horizon, and he pushed Caoimhe to go faster.

She seemed to catch his mood, and glanced uneasily around her. "What is wrong, Ailill?"

"Nothing, love. All is well." He smiled down at her, trying to reassure her.

"I wouldn't count on that," sneered a voice from the gathering shadows.

CHAPTER FIVE

Aisling was beginning to feel more relaxed around Fergal. An afternoon spent wandering the Faire, her wings once more securely hidden, had served to bring them closer together. As they walked hand in hand, he shared his dreams with her.

"Someday, I will have a grand workshop, with a band of apprentices to which I'll teach my craft. We'll be sought after by all the nobles to create leather goods for their castles. My name will be known far and wide, and my mark will be found in the Court of the King!"

"It sounds wondrous, Fergal," she breathed. "You are a true artisan." She fingered the pouch at her waist. "I wish I could make such beauty."

"You are beauty enough," he answered, dropping a kiss on her upturned nose.

She giggled. "'Tis a quicksilver tongue you have, Fergal O'Connor and no mistake."

"So, there be the two of you, hand in hand like sweethearts. 'Tis as I feared." The old man who had given the twins their gold coins stood before them in the pathway, arms akimbo.

Fergal glowered back. "And there you be, you old menace. You frightened my Aisling here to death with your foolish blather. Aisling, this is my grandfather, Seamus O'Connor."

"Aisling is it? And a vision she is indeed." The old man's face broke into a broad grin, and he stepped forward to take Aisling's hand in his. He raised it to his lips and kissed it gallantly. "Well come to our hamlet, Aisling." He punched Fergal's arm lightly. "I should have known it would be you to steal her heart, you rascal."

"Don't try your nonsense on me, old man. You knew all along we would find each other...but why did you make it sound like a curse? I have never been so happy in my life. For the first time in my life, I have found someone I could spend forever with."

The old man's seamed face creased into a mask of pain. "If only it could be so easy, lad. Come, let us go where we can talk freely."

He threaded his way through the thinning market crowd, leading them to a small neat cottage set back from the main street of town. Inside the one room dwelling, he gestured Aisling to a seat near the banked fire. Fussing about the room, he soon had the fire crackling in the grate and a kettle steaming on the hook.

"Sit down, Fergal, lad. There is much to discuss."

Fergal sat down beside Aisling at the table, reaching out and taking her hand in his. "Tell us what you have to say, Grand-da."

The old man sighed. "The world of the Fae and that of we mortals are never supposed to merge. It takes a sacrifice beyond price to create such a union. Are you both prepared to make such a sacrifice?"

"What are you talking about, old one?" Fergal murmured. "What sacrifice?"

"Aisling, my dear," Seamus said gently, taking her other hand in both of his. "Do you realize what it would mean to give your heart to a mortal?"

Aisling felt her heart contract. "I fear it is too late to consider it," she whispered.

"He is young and strong now, but he will one day age and die as do we all. You are ageless and timeless. The Fae live forever unless they will otherwise, and you cease to age at maturity. Soon, as the course of these things go, he would pass you up and begin to fail before your eyes. What will you do then?"

"I do no' know, sir." She felt her lip tremble, and tears spring into her eyes. "I had no' thought..."

"And you, Fergal, lad. When you begin to age, and feel your strength wane while your lady stays young and fair, will you begin to resent her? Can you stay in love when she is changeless?"

Fergal's face grew dark. "I would hope I am no' so shallow as that."

"'Tis not shallow, lad. 'Tis truthfulness. You cannot be faulted for the truth. There is only one chance for this to last, and the decision must not be made lightly. You have only this day met. Before you decide to take such an irreversible step, you must weigh all possibilities."

"What do you mean?" asked Aisling, her voice a mere whisper.

"For such a relationship to flourish, you must renounce your Fae blood and choose the mortal way. The only way to achieve this is to go to the White Lady and beg her intervention. If you plead your case and she grants your boon, you will lose your wings and become mortal. You will nevermore be able to walk the hills of Faerie."

Aisling gulped, looking over at Fergal. "I would do so for my Lord," she breathed.

"I could no' let you make a sacrifice so grand," Fergal protested. "To lose eternity for the likes of me?"

"What is eternity if I have no one to share it with? In a century, I have no' found a soul to make my heart sing as you have done. If it means I shed my wings, I do it gladly."

Fergal came to stand behind Aisling, his arm around her shoulders offering comfort and protection. "I will no' let you go alone."

"Of course not," agreed Seamus. "You must go at her side. The White Lady is the Queen of the Dead. Only she can give Aisling the gift of death. It is a long and arduous journey. The end is not guaranteed."

Aisling laid her hand on Fergal's. "What must I do?"

"Time enough tomorrow. It is too late to start out tonight. Aisling, you must stay here this night. Tomorrow you will start out at daybreak. I will gather provisions for the journey while you rest. Fergal, go you and close up your house and shop. I will watch your lady and keep her safe while you are gone."

Fergal nodded and then took Aisling into his arms. He hugged her tightly, taking care not to smash her wings. "I will cherish you for all my days, Aisling. Such a sacrifice should not be made lightly. If you are sure you wish to do this, I will follow at your side to the ends of the earth. But I would stay with you until the end of my days whether you make this decision or no'."

Aisling looked up into his face. "I will spend my life with you Fergal O'Connor, and go down to the land of the dead when you go thither."

Seamus put one hand on each of their shoulders. "This is a union meant to be. But it will be hard won. Go now, Fergal. Aisling needs her rest."

"Aye. I'll return shortly." He kissed her hard, and then he was gone.

Aisling remained, staring after him. "Will it hurt, Seamus?"

"'Tis likely, lass. If she will grant you audience. The White Lady is fickle in her attentions."

Aisling snatched her wings free of their confinement. "I wish I could tear them from my back and be done with it!"

Seamus soothed her. "Lambling, it would not help to hurt yourself so. Your wings are a glorious gift, and so is eternity. I ask you again, without Fergal to hear. Are you sure you are willing to make this sacrifice? 'Twould be better for you both if you returned to your hill, and let the memory of this day slip into the shadows."

"I cannot. When I met you this morning, you told me I would lose my heart. Well, I have. I cannot think of life alone after meeting Fergal. I would no' wish to live beyond him."

Seamus smiled. "I merely wanted to be sure, lass. I can see the truth shining inside of you. You were meant to be together. Even the Lady must bow before the power of such love."

Aisling's wings beat nervously, lifting her an inch or two above the floor.

"What is it like, to fly?"

"I really can't remember. All my wings can do now is lift me for a space of time. I am grown too large. The hatchlings flit about like birds, but once we come to full growth, our mass outweighs what the wings can lift, and we are tethered to the earth the same as you. I would say 'twas like jumping very high and staying aloft for a heartbeat more than you expect." She smiled at him. "Is that an answer?"

"Aye, lass. So you won't regret it when your wings are clipped?"

"No' for the sake of Fergal."

"I believe you, Aisling. You have convinced me. It seems strange you can be so sure after so short an acquaintance, but stranger things have been known."

She felt a yawn rising from the center of her and tried to stave it off. Her attempt was only partly successful, and she tried to hide the result behind her hand.

"You are tired," Seamus scolded. "I should not keep you, blathering like this. It has been a long day for you, child. Come and lie down here beside the fire. You will need to be rested on the morrow."

He guided her to the narrow cot beside the fire and bade her make herself comfortable. Gently, he covered her with a light blanket, taking care for her wings.

His lips brushed her forehead, and she noticed sleepily his kiss felt quite different from Fergal's. "Good night, my Lady Fae," whispered Seamus.

"Good night," she murmured in reply, her eyelids already drifting closed.

As she sank down into the arms of slumber, she heard Seamus pottering about the cottage, and a sense of peace cocooned her. She felt safe here, safer than she had ever known. A brief flash of anxiety threatened to lift her back to wakefulness when she thought of Ailill, and wondered where he had gone, but the anchor of sleep was too heavy, and she was dragged back under.

She regretted that they had parted badly, and quarrelling at that, but there would be another day to sort out those feelings. He was, after all, her twin, and they shared a bond nothing could break. She only hoped one day he would find such happiness of his own and forgive her for what she planned to do.

Her thoughts drifted ever deeper into the bowels of sleep. The noises Seamus made were translated into the sounds she associated with home, and she began to dream of her family aerie in the barrow. Mother would be placing food upon the table while Father tended to his bow. The hatchlings would be flitting about getting underfoot, and Ailill would be teasing their older brother who would soon move into a home of his own with his sweetheart.

It was the only life she had ever known or had thought to ever know. But now her thoughts turned to a small stone cottage, with Fergal's dark head bent over his work as he crafted a leather bracer. She saw herself standing at the hearth, stirring a pot above the fire, her face a little older; worn, but happy. She saw a pair of children tussling over a scrap of leather at Fergal's feet and heard his hearty laugh as he swept his work aside and lifted them both into his lap. They squealed with delight as he mock-scolded them for interrupting his work.

This was the life she could have if the White Lady was merciful...though the thought of meeting that dread being made her moan in her sleep. The Lady was often cruel. Her whims were legendary. She could decide to help the lovers or, just as easily, refuse for spite. The Lady was high in the Unseelie Court and a sworn enemy to their King. Would she help despite the feud? Aisling couldn't guess.

Chapter Six

"Darragh! What are you doing skulking about so close to nightfall?" Ailill stepped in front of Caoimhe, shielding her with his wings as he confronted his elder brother.

"I might ask you the same, witless fool. Where is Aisling? Who is this wingless one, and why have you brought her here? You know the law."

Ailill raised his chin defiantly. "I don't know where Aisling is. She is old enough to know her own mind. As for Caoimhe, I would vouch for her with my life." He heard a gasp from the lady in question but did not turn.

"And well you might have to. 'Tis lucky you are 'tis I on patrol this eve. Go you at once to the aerie, and get out of sight before one of the King's men sees you. Father will have much to say about this matter."

Ailill swallowed hard. "I have no doubt of *that*," he muttered under his breath. He was not looking forward to what his proud father *would* say on the subject. "Come, Caoimhe, we'd best do as he says."

He took her hand in his, not surprised to find it was like holding onto a ball of snow. He glanced down and saw her face pale and set but her shoulders back and her carriage straight. She might be terrified, but she wouldn't show it. What a magnificent lass she was!

"You had better be able to explain yourself," Darragh commented. "It won't help that you seem to have lost Aisling along the way, either."

"We are no' children, Darragh, and it is time we are recognized as grown. The entire Court clucks over our lack of responsibility and then sends us off with the hatchlings if there are matters of importance to discuss. There is no one within a quarter century young or old of our age since the ravages of winter three years ago. When there are none for us to bond with in Faerie, is it any wonder our eyes look out?"

"I am no' the one to answer. You must convince the Council, no' I. I am merely a Warder and happy to be so. Go your way now before I am missed in my patrol." He turned and walked away from them, disappearing into the dusk before he had gone a dozen paces.

Ailill glanced up at the sky. The sun had completely disappeared save for a shaving of gold above the horizon, and the clouds were already trading their orange and crimson finery for the purple and black of night. "'Tis later than I realized. We'd best run from here. Are you up to it?" he asked Caoimhe.

She nodded, the movement barely discernable in the growing dark. "I think so."

"'Tisn't far," he promised. "And the path is smooth."

They began to run.

He heard a muffled exclamation at one point and felt her stumble, but he could not afford to let them stop. The distance to the aerie seemed to have stretched like a worn bowstring. Would they never reach it?

Ailill was on the verge of giving up when the home tree loomed up before him. Firefly lanterns hung in all the branches. Their light was dim but enough to illuminate the steps spiraling up the trunk of the ancient oak. The steps were narrow, protruding mere inches from the tree. Meant for Faerie folk who stabilized themselves with their wings as they climbed, they posed a problem for Caoimhe.

"I can't climb those!" she protested. "Ailill, I shall fall. They can never hold me up."

"They are sturdier than they look, love—just as you. I will climb behind you if you like, to steady you if you start to fall."

"I-I'll try."

He could see her trembling, though the light grew ever dimmer. "That's my brave girl," he encouraged her. "Up you go. 'Twill be over in no time."

Caoimhe put her little bare foot on the first step and started to climb, hugging the trunk of the tree as closely as she might.

Ailill stayed right behind her, ready to catch her if she lost her balance. In truth, he hovered beside the stairs instead of resting on them as he might normally because he could more easily block her fall if she slipped.

By the time they reached the landing outside the aerie, both of them were exhausted. Ailill's wings were thrumming with the exertion of the climb. He caught her hand and raised it to his lips.

"Well done, my beauty."

Caoimhe smiled weakly. "Thank you, my Lord. I—oh!"

He chuckled, seeing the rapt wonder on her face as she gazed upon the spires of the Faerie city. "Is it no' beautiful?"

All around them, the trees were graced with the aeries of the Sidhe. Tall towers of crystal seemed to be spun from moonbeams. The light of the firefly lanterns reflected off the crystal in a pearly glow while the brighter golden illumination of torchlight streamed from the windows.

"We should get inside," Ailill said gently, regret coloring his words. "'Tis better swiftly done."

Caoimhe shuddered and then squared her shoulders. "As you say. I am ready."

He pulled her into his arms and planted a swift kiss on her parted lips. "My brave darling... Do no' worry. I will protect you. This I swear."

He reached around her and pressed the hidden knot to open the door. Despite his words, he felt his stomach clench in anticipation of his father's wrath.

The door swept silently open, and a burst of light and sound swelled around them.

"Ailill! Ailill!" The cries of the hatchlings as they swarmed around him were shrill and exuberant. The tiny beings darted around their heads and rested on his shoulders, staring wide-eyed at Caoimhe.

One of the boldest hovered before the mortal's face, peering intently at her. "What is this?" hissed the boy, his wings beating madly. "She's no Fae."

One of the girl hatchlings tugged on Ailill's hair and whispered in his ear.

Ailill laughed aloud. "No, little one. She will no' eat you."

Caoimhe's face grew red.

"Ailill!" roared a voice from the room beyond, and the hatchlings scattered with squeals of dismay.

Ailill took a deep breath, and held out his hand to Caoimhe.

Wordlessly, she placed her own in his, and together they walked into the fray.

The main chamber of the aerie was a circular room hollowed out of the great tree. As they entered, the hatchlings settled onto perches around the top of the room. A brazier in the center of the chamber sent up perfumed smoke to waft out of vents in the ceiling. The room was warm and radiated comfort.

At the far side of the brazier, in a throne-like chair carved from a single block of oak, sat his father, Eoghan. Hair as fair as moonlight fell in a braid over one shoulder to his waist. A circlet of silver, as was his right as King's kin, rested upon his brow. His face was set in a frown as they entered the room.

"Where have you been, boy? And where is your sister? Your mother—what is this? You dare to bring a mortal past the gate! Where are your wits?"

Ailill gulped but held his ground. "I left Aisling in the market square. She would no' come. 'Tis no' my place to force her. She is a woman grown."

"Only when her actions suit the title. When she behaves like a hatchling, she shall be treated like one. And you as well. You compromise us all by bringing this doxy here."

Ailill's fear burned away in a tide of anger. "How dare you speak of Caoimhe so! She is a lady, no' a common trollop."

"How would you know?" sneered Eoghan. "You base this claim on an acquaintance of what—a summer's day? 'Tis one thing to sport amongst the mortals. Even I have dallied so in my time. But to risk the wrath of King and Court to bring one inside the barrow...by the gods, have I raised a simpleton?"

"Nay, Father. I am no dolt. I am come of age and able to make my own decisions."

"So say you?" The Fae lord rose to his feet, towering

over them. His voice thundered. "Fine. 'Tis all one to me. Get you gone from my house. You are no longer welcome here. As of this day, you are no son to me. And if your sister cares not for home, she can be damned as well!"

Ailill stared at his father. He had not expected the proud Fae to accept Caoimhe with open arms, but neither had he expected the reception to be so harsh. "You can't mean that," he whispered.

"That and more. If you and your...lady—" His tone made the honorific a condemnation. "—dare to return to the aerie, I will call down the guard upon you."

Ailill took a half step toward his father, and Eoghan turned his back upon his son.

"Fine!" Ailill felt his temper surge. They would do fine without the family. They would be their *own* family.

Ailill snatched his bow and quiver from their resting place against the wall. "You are the fool, old one. You have lived too long to remember what it feels to love. I pity you."

"Get out!"

Ailill shepherded Caoimhe out the door and into the entryway.

"Oh, Ailill—" she began.

"Hush, love. 'Twas no' your fault. Stubborn old fool..."

"Ailill..." The voice spoke his name softly, with a discernable edge of sorrow.

He turned. In the shadows of the entryway stood his mother, Ailidh, a leaf-wrapped packet in one hand. He had never noticed before how slight and fragile she was. Her hair was the russet of Aisling's, but threads of silver wound through it, glittering in the half-light. There was a sadness in her green eyes that tore at his heart, but he could do nothing to change it.

She reached up to touch first his cheek and then Caoimhe's. "I see much love in your eyes," she murmured, voice wistful. "I hope you will be happy, though I fear it will not be easy. You must choose. One of you must give up all you hold dear for the sake of the other." Her voice caught, and she took a deep breath before continuing.

"I would hope you choose to stay here in Faerie with us, my dear." She smiled sadly at Caoimhe. "If the King decrees it, it may be so, and he is sometimes sympathetic to lovers."

Ailidh turned to Ailill. "You will have to seek his blessing, my son."

She pressed the packet into his hand. "Here is waybread and a bit of honey. It will help sustain you on your journey." She hesitated then went on. "What of your sister? Do you know where she has gone?"

"I left her in the marketplace," he mumbled, eyes downcast. "She met a mortal man, and I chided her for her foolishness."

He heard Caoimhe's gasp behind him and turned to her. "I had no' laid eyes upon you yet, beloved, and I did no' understand. Now I know what she must have felt. I can only wish her well and hope her happiness is as great as my own."

Ailidh sighed. "Neither road is a happy one, my son. But what is done is done. I wish her peace. I fear I shall not see her again." A tear slid slowly down her cheek. "You were always my stubborn children. Set apart from the moment of birth. But you are two halves of a whole. You must stay in contact with Aisling, Ailill. Neither of you will be content unless you do."

He bent and hugged her tightly. "I will do as you say, Mother. I will no' abandon her."

"Good. I knew I could trust you for that." She pushed him away gently. "Now, get you gone. If your father finds out you are still here, he will go mad."

She opened the door and shooed them out onto the landing. "Go to the King. Be your most eloquent, Ailill. You can talk the birds from the skies. Convince him."

Turning one final time to Caoimhe, she slipped a ring from off her finger. "Take this, my dear," she said, pressing the trinket into the girl's hand. "It will keep you safe in time of need."

"T-thank you, my Lady," murmured Caoimhe, dropping into a curtsey. "I will treasure it always."

"Now go." His mother jerked her head at the stairway as she closed the door. "It is no longer safe for you to stay."

Slinging his bow and quiver across his back, Ailill led the way down the tree. The confrontation with his father had shaken him badly. Family was all to the Fae, and now he had lost his. His sharp hearing caught the faint scrape of Caoimhe's foot against a step as she followed him down the tree, and he bit his lip. Was he doing the right thing? Was it worth losing everything for a girl—and a mortal one at that—he had only just met?

When they reached the bottom safely, Caoimhe threw herself into his arms, sobs wracking her slender shoulders. As his arms tightened around her, he knew the answer to his question. This was worth everything. They would be their own family now.

"Where will we go, Ailill? I'm frightened."

"Hush, lass," he soothed, stroking her silky hair. "All will be well."

"How can it be? I've gotten you disowned, and it's the middle of the night, and..."

He chuckled. "Come, come. It's no so late as that. And if I had a sovereign for every time my father cast me out, I'd be a rich man," he lied.

"Where will we sleep?"

"I have an uncle no' far from here known to look at things a bit less conventionally. I am sure he will grant us space for the night, and on the morrow, we will seek an audience with the King. The King is wise and kind. He will see how much I love you, and he will grant our petition. All will be well. I promise."

She shuddered in his arms. "If you say it will, it must be so."

"Aye. Now come. Let us find a roof for the night."

With his arm around her shoulders, he walked away from the only home he had ever known. He didn't look back.

CHAPTER SEVEN

The faint flush of dawn was seeping through the shutters when Aisling's eyes fluttered open. A surge of terror engulfed her, and she started upright before remembering where she was and how she had come to be here. The thought of Fergal sent a wave of happiness through her to wash away her fright, and she looked around her with renewed interest.

Seamus' cottage was neat as a pin. Its one room was utilitarian but filled with homey touches that revealed its owner's personality. The cot on which she sat was covered with a thick blanket dyed a lovely russet. A beautifully carved chest sat against the far wall, and a cracked mug filled with pretty dried grasses and colorful autumn leaves rested in the middle of the well-scrubbed table. Slumped over the table, head pillowed on crossed arms, Fergal still slept.

A smile curved her lips. He looked so young and vulnerable with his hair tousled from sleep.

"Handsome lad, no?" asked a soft voice at her elbow, and she jumped.

"I did no mean to scare you, lass," Seamus murmured with a chuckle. He continued stirring the pot he had hung over the fire. "There will be porridge soon to break your fast."

"Thank you," she replied, nodding her head gratefully. The half-eaten meat pie at yesterday's nooning was long gone, and she was ravenous.

"While the boy sleeps, I must ask you something,

Lady Aisling...and I bid you speak true..."

"What is it?" A sinking sensation began in the pit of her stomach, and she swallowed hard, no longer certain she wanted food.

"You have no worked any of your Fae magic on my lad there, have you? He is all I have left in the world, and I would not see you play with his heart for sport."

Aisling was taken aback. No one had ever doubted her honesty or character before. Such a question would have been unheard of among the Fae. Using magic without another's knowledge was considered the height of uncivilized, and to accuse someone of doing so was a grave insult indeed. "No! I swear it. I want only what he cares to give. I would no' for the world cause him pain or bring him harm."

Seamus sighed. "You may not be able to help it. If you go forth to seek the White Lady, he may well come to harm. The Unseelie Court is filled with jealous souls, as well you know."

"You fear for him."

"I fear for you both."

"What must I do?" Her voice came out as a mere thread of sound. She feared to hear his response.

"If you truly love him as you say, save him from himself. Get you gone before he wakes. Then, if you do indeed crave this boon from the White Lady, and she complies, come back to him a mortal. Do not make him go with you on this journey. Think what would happen if he were caught up in the Unseelie Court."

Aisling felt her heart catch in her breast. "Aye. You are right. The White Lady and her huntsman would destroy him. I-I must go alone."

Seamus took her hand in his. "I knew you were a special lass. I will keep him safe for you."

Tears threatened to blind her, but she nodded her head bravely. "I will hurry." Without a second thought, she ran out of the cottage, unable to bear another glance at Fergal.

* * *

Fergal woke sometime later with a stretch and a yawn. His dreams had been filled with visions much like Aisling's: a home, hearth and children playing. He was eager to start on their quest so he could begin making those dreams a reality. He glanced around the cottage. His heart sank when he saw she was not there.

Seamus sat on the edge of her cot, stirring a pot simmering on the fire.

"Where is Aisling, Grand-da?"

"She's gone, lad."

Fergal's heart stopped beating. "W-what do you mean, 'she's gone'?"

"She left." Seamus shrugged. "'Tis the way of the Fae. They are a flighty sort."

"Aisling would never leave without saying good-bye at least. What did you say to her?"

"I said nothing. She was gone ere I woke."

Fergal's eyes narrowed. He knew firsthand the trickery Seamus was capable of. "You are lying, old man. What are you hiding from me?"

"There is nothing to hide. When I awoke, your bird had flown. Perhaps she thought again about giving up her wings and freedom. Perhaps she merely jested with you. Whatever the case, she is out of your life and well rid of her you are."

Fergal surged to his feet, knocking over his stool in the process. "You are a doddering old fool. I love her, Grand-da. Can you no live with that?"

"You only met her yesterday noon. How can you talk of love?"

"Love is no' a measured, plodding thing. It comes as it likes and strikes with the swiftness of lightning. She holds my heart, and if she has gone, then my soul is gone with her."

"You sound like a lack-wit schoolboy," Seamus scoffed. "You are better off without the chit."

Fergal could feel the blood pounding in his temples, and he took a deep breath to calm himself before he spoke. "If I believed for one moment you meant what you just said, old man, it would be the last words you ever spoke to me."

Seamus met his gaze squarely and then seemed to fold in on himself. He sighed heavily. "I hoped to keep you safe, lad. It's all I've ever wanted to do. 'Tis true, she is no flighty Fae. But 'tis also true she is gone. She seeks the White Lady alone."

"How could you do this?" Fergal exploded. "How could you let her go without me?"

"You have no idea what you would have been up against, boy. The White Lady is the Queen of Demons. She eats the hearts of mortal men to break her fast. I could not let you go into that danger. Not for the world. Not even for love."

"'Twas no your choice to make. How dare you!" Fergal began to pace the confines of the dwelling like a caged cat. "You had no right to let her go alone. If anything happens to her—"

"For what it matters, I am sorry, Fergal. I had no idea you felt so strongly. It did no' seem possible you could love so deep after so short an acquaintance. She has no' been gone long. If you hurry, you mayhaps could catch her up outside of town."

Fergal snatched his jacket and cap. "I had better find her, old man, or it is you who will pay the price." He jammed his cap upon his head and stalked out of the cottage.

* * *

Aisling fled into the strengthening sunlight with no thought to direction. She was sobbing as if her heart was broken, and indeed, it felt as if it were. She had never in her life been alone. Ailill had always been by her side—aye, sometimes a bully—but there to shore her up if she should sag. She felt lost and powerless.

How could she convince the White Lady, the Queen of Demons, to grant a request to a foolish stripling Sidhe, not to mention a member of the rival Court? What was she to do? She could not lose Fergal now she had found him...and if it meant giving up her immortality then so be it.

So blinded was she by her tears, she did not see the man until she ran squarely into his chest. Suddenly, hard, rough hands grabbed her arms and held her fast.

She looked up, and realized, with a thrill of terror, that she had left the cottage in such a hurry she had left behind her disguise, poor as it was. She tried to struggle free of the man's grasp, but it was deceptively light.

"Wha' have we here? A pretty little vixen..."

She saw the dawning realization light his eyes as his glance darted to her wings and then to her pointed ears and odd clothing.

"No," he breathed, "not a vixen. A pixie! A Faerie witch come to steal our babes as they sleep in their cradles. To sour the milk and drive the horses mad."

Aisling froze in terror. She opened her mouth to protest, but not a squeak of sound came out.

"We don't truck with your like in our town," he grated, breath foul with stale beer and garlic. "We deal harsh with witches here."

"B-but I'm no—"

"Keep your tongue still in your head, witch! I'll let the magistrate decide. He'll do me proud for saving the town from trash like you." His fingers tightened in anticipation of his reward, and Aisling whimpered. "Hush your whining. 'Twon't help you in the end."

Aisling pulled desperately against his hold, her wings beating frantically as she tried to escape. The tip of one wing caught the man across the face, leaving a shallow cut.

He bellowed with rage and cuffed her hard.

She half-swooned from the blow.

He dragged her through the streets, and she struggled to keep her feet under her, only partially succeeding. After an interminable age, he stopped before a large, well-built dwelling, which boasted an upper floor. He pounded on the door with one fist, the other wrapped securely around Aisling's slender arm.

A window on the top floor swung open, and a

disgruntled voice called down. "What is the racket? It is early morn yet. The magistrate ain't hearing petitions until noon."

"He'll hear mine, I reckon," the man bellowed back. "I caught one of them Fae demons skulking along in our very streets!"

There was a gasp from the window above. "You don't say! Truth you're telling?"

"I swear it."

"I'll tell him right away. Stay right there."

Her captor smirked at Aisling. "We'll soon see about you, girlie." He reached out and pinched her wing cruelly between thumb and forefinger. "Why, 'tis like paper! Such a wing is never good for flying. What weak, pathetic creatures the mighty Fae."

Aisling felt her panic beginning to burn away under a clear, cold hatred. This man was a bully like Daragh. He would never dare treat her like this if he knew the true extent of Fae powers. Maybe she should teach him a lesson...

...but it was too late. The door sprang open, and a well-dressed man stood in the doorway, exuding authority.

"What have we here, O'Hanlon?"

The man who had captured her tugged off his cap and bowed before the magistrate. "I-I caught this here Fae witch near the market, M'lord. I think she was here to wreak havoc on our village."

"Indeed? And why would she want to do such a thing?"

"Who knows why the Fae do anything, your lordship?" O'Hanlon shrugged. "What will you do to her?"

"That is a question for the court to decide," answered

his lordship with a yawn. "Leave her with me, and go your way."

O'Hanlon protested. "She's mine! I found her fair and square."

"And I will see you are compensated for your trouble. Unless you remain to provoke me, and then I will see to it your life is just as abysmal as hers. Possibly more so."

O'Hanlon blanched then dropped Aisling's arm at last. "As you say, my Lord. I leave her to you." He shoved Aisling in the small of her back, and she fell into the hallway at the magistrate's feet.

"Run along, O'Hanlon," ordered the magistrate with a wave of his hand.

"But what about—?"

"I said I would see you compensated. Now go."

O' Hanlon shuffled off down the street, muttering over his shoulder.

Aisling lay where she had fallen, too terrified to rise. Her eyes focused on the inlay pattern of the hallway floor. There was wealth here, and where there was wealth, there was usually power. What would that power mean to her?

She felt a soft hand encircle her arm and make as if to lift her to her feet. She let out a stifled cry as the magistrate inadvertently put pressure on the bruises O'Hanlon had left on her bicep.

The magistrate clucked sympathetically. "Well, then, my dear. You will have to rise of your own accord."

Trembling all over, Aisling managed to stagger to her feet. Her wings curled protectively about her shoulders.

"Well, now, lass. What shall we do with you?"

CHAPTER EIGHT

Their reception had been less than Ailill hoped for when they knocked at his Uncle Cian's door. The stooped Fae, as ancient as the hill he lived beneath, had scolded Ailill roundly, leaving him red-faced and trembling with rage at being so rebuked before Caoimhe.

She pretended nothing was amiss, not wanting to add to his discomfiture.

It was only with great reluctance, and on condition they would leave at first light, they had gotten a bed at all. Now, the sun was rising in the west, and Cian was waiting to speed them on their way.

"'Tis a fool you are, Ailill Brightwing, and a fool you've always been." He turned a cold, silver stare on Caoimhe. "To call down your father's wrath for a girl—and a mortal one at that! You would be best served to take her back from whence she came, and forget you ever set eyes upon her."

Ailill slipped a supportive arm around Caoimhe's shoulders. "I love her, Uncle. I truly thought you, of all, would understand."

"What do you intend to do with her? Keep her as a pet until she grows old and gray and then find yourself another?"

"I plan to petition the King for the gift of an apple."

Cian's face grew bloodless. "Do no' even jest of such, boy!"

"I do *not* jest. I am perfectly serious."

"You cannot do it!"

"I can, and I shall."

Caoimhe laid a hand on Ailill's sleeve. "What do you speak of, Ailill?"

He turned to her and took her hands, gazing deep into her eyes. "I will petition the King for one of the golden apples from his sacred tree. The apples grant the boon of eternal life. You can become immortal and live forever at my side, here in Faerie. We will build our own aerie, and our hatchlings will fill the skies."

"And if they have no wings?"

"Then they will run like the wind and still out-distance their flying cousins." He smiled down at her. "Will you stay with me, Caoimhe?"

Cian snorted. "Do no' offer the prize before it is won, stripling. The King may well deny your request."

Ailill stood up to his uncle. "When he sees the beauty of my Caoimhe's face, and hears the wisdom of her soul, he will be happy to grant my request, old one. And if you and my father cannot see past your own noses then we are well rid of your council."

He turned back to the girl. "What is your answer?"

* * *

Caoimhe stared at Ailill in shock. Was he serious? He was offering her immortality? Everlasting youth and the bliss of Faerie? Her mind reeled. It was a gift beyond price. How *could* she accept? She had met him yester morn and not under the best of circumstances. To contemplate accepting him would be foolishness. And yet, she found herself saying, "Yes. If the King will grant your boon, I will accept the gift, Ailill Brightwing..."

The name suited him. She had not known it until Cian's condemnation, but 'Brightwing' was the perfect appellation for Ailill. *Her* Ailill...that sounded right as well. She could not think of returning to the barren, wasted life she had lived before their unexpected meeting in the market.

His face lit with joy as her acceptance sank in. He grabbed her around the waist and began to spin. She was laughing so hard it took her a moment to realize they were floating about three feet off the floor. She gasped in surprise.

"Oh, Ailill...I'm flying!"

"As we shall ever fly together, my love."

"Get out of my sight," ordered Cian. "I will have no more truck with you. You have gone beyond foolishness into madness, and I will no' be a part of it."

She could feel Ailill trembling like a restless colt.

"Let me down," she said quietly.

He obeyed, the landing abrupt and heavy. His wings sagged, and he fought to hide his windedness.

She laid a hand on his cheek and smiled. "Thank you, beloved." Then she turned to Cian, drawing herself up to her full height.

"I am sorry you do no' approve of me, sir. Mayhaps in time your opinion can be altered, but whether it may be or no, I will no' leave him. I pledge Ailill my life, with you as witness. You and the rest of the clan had best become used to it."

She turned and walked out of the house without waiting for an answer. Inwardly, her heart was pounding like a drum, but she refused to let the old Fae see how rattled she was. She had her pride, and it was the only dowry she brought to the table, so she would not compromise it.

She heard Ailill coming after her but didn't stop until she was well clear of the dwelling. She felt his hand on her shoulder and finally turned toward him.

His face was alight, and his voice was filled with wonder as he murmured, "What have I gone and gotten myself into? You were magnificent, beloved. I am no' worthy of the likes of you!"

She laughed ruefully, swiping away tears even as others slipped beyond her control to trace her cheekbones. "I-I am sorry, Ailill. You shall have no family left ere long, and 'tis all my fault."

"No' a bit of it!" He hugged her tight. "My family has never known what to do with me. I have ever been the bad seed of the household. Aisling has kept what little place I had intact for me. They would have found cause eventually to be rid of me without your coming."

He dropped a kiss on her forehead. "Come. We go to see the King and seek our boon."

"Will he grant it, Ailill?"

"I cannot say for certain. He is wayward in his fancies at times. But there is a good chance that loyal service and promised toil will sway his heart." His face lost all animation. "If no', I shall scale the orchard wall and take what I need."

Caoimhe gasped. "You will do no such thing! Such a rare gift freely given is one thing, and I will accept it with all my heart to be at your side forever. But such a gift stolen from the royal orchard—it would be tainted from the start. Where could we go after such a crime? Your wings preclude you coming to my world, and you would be hunted like a thief in Faerie. No, my love. If the King refuses your petition then 'tis an end on it. I will no' be party to such. I'll have your word on that!"

"As you say, beloved," answered Ailill meekly, but she sensed evasion in his tone. She would have to watch him closely and make sure he lived up to his vow.

* * *

The sun was nearing its zenith when the lovers came at last to the crystal palace rising from its sheltering lake. A shimmering wall of diamond encompassed most of the island encircling the castle and grounds. A carpet of thick, emerald grass washed up against the wall in gently billowing waves, a second sea inside the lake. Delicate spires and turrets reached up into the sky, and pennants of crimson and gold snapped in the breeze. The sound of distant shouts carried to them where they stood beside the lake, and the aromas of a large stronghold—baking bread, roasting meat, middens, stables, and all—wafted across the water.

Ailill turned to Caoimhe. "Behold the walls of Avalon, home to Avallach, Dagda of the Sidhe. His cauldron is never empty, and his children are legion. His orchard houses the golden apples of eternal youth. He is the ruler of the Seelie Court, and all in Fae stand in awe of him."

"Maybe we shouldn't have come," she whispered nervously. "Why would such a mighty King deign to speak to such as we?"

"Because his door is always open to those in need, and his largesse flows freely. I would say we qualify."

She smiled weakly at his joke.

"Besides, I have done him service a time or two, and I feel confident he will remember and grant my request." *Or have me thrown in irons for asking.*

"I am no' dressed to appear before a King," Caoimhe fretted, ineffectually smoothing her apron. "I look like a common farmer's daughter. I know in truth I *am*, but I would have hidden such from a King."

"You are beautiful, beloved. The King will see beyond your dress to your heart, as I have done."

"I fear you are biased, my love. But if you say 'tis well..."

"Trust me, Caoimhe. I will no' let you come to harm." *If it means my life...*

Taking her hand in his, he strode firmly up to the narrow causeway leading to the castle. In times of turmoil, the drawbridge would be raised, and the lake itself would serve as moat. For now, the bridge was down, completing the span of common lands to castle.

Ailill moved as if he owned the keep. Shoulders proudly back and wings spread, he marched forward. It was a bold move, and he was nearly at the gate before they were challenged.

"Halt!" commanded a grim-faced guard in silver and blue livery. "State your purpose with the Dagda."

Ailill sketched a bow. "Ailill Brightwing, son of Eoghan, kinsman to the King. I seek audience on a private matter."

"I know your name. As I do your father's, whelp. And I have seen him pass inside this day in a state of rage with your name attached to it. It will avail you little to seek the King today."

"I must speak to the King!"

The guard, who had been focusing his attention on Ailill, suddenly spied Caoimhe behind the Fae. His face darkened, and a glowering frown drew the corners of his mouth. "What is this, lack-wit? You bring a mortal wench to the heart of the Seelie Court? Are you mad?"

"My business is with Avallach and no with the likes of you."

"Keep a civil tongue in your head, boy! Do you know the penalty for bringing a mortal into Faerie? This could cost your head."

Caoimhe moaned, and Ailill tightened his grip on her hand to reassure her.

"I am sure the Dagda will have something to say about that," he asserted. "I will speak to him about it, and no one else."

"Then you will speak to no one because the Dagda bears no truck with mortals. As for this one..." The guard seized Caoimhe's upper arm. "We will give her a place in Faerie all right." He sneered down at her, his eyes cold silver beads. "She will no' be our guest long."

"Let her go. Get your hands off of her!" Ailill started forward.

The guard pushed him back with a hard shove to the center of his chest. "Go home, boy. You are no' needed here."

Ailill rose slowly to his feet. He could feel the blood pounding in his temples. "Let her go!"

"Ailill!" Caoimhe cried, her terror palpable.

"I said, let her go!"

The guard cuffed him across the face, knocking him to the pathway, and splitting his lip. "And I said go home, boy. You are no' wanted here. Things will be worse for you both if you do no' do as you are bid."

Before Ailill could scramble to his feet once more, the guard had dragged Caoimhe into the shadows of the guard tower.

"Watch him," he commanded to the two guards on either side of the causeway. "Do no' let him through the gate."

Ailill started forward, but the two guards stepped together to block the gateway. Each had their hand on the hilt of a nasty looking sword.

"Caoimhe!" he cried in frustration.

"Ailill!"

"I will find you—I swear it."

And then she was gone, dragged into the inner keep and out of his sight.

CHAPTER NINE

Aisling dared look up at last and gasped with surprise.

The magistrate stared back at her with hooded eyes the color of twilight. A half-smile quirked his lip while the silver hair hanging about his shoulders did not quite disguise the tips of his ears. "Hello there, little one. I doubt you remember me. You were no more than a hatchling when I saw you last. What were you doing to go and get yourself brought before the law?"

Aisling felt faint. She must be imagining things. "I know no' what you mean, sir."

"Please, come and sit." He gestured her toward a room off the hallway. It was furnished with delicate wooden furniture in a style reminiscent of growing saplings. The upholstery was all soft spring greens and watered blues.

It reminded Aisling of a woodland bower. She sank down onto one of the chairs with relief, curling her feet under her automatically before remembering she was not at home in the aerie. With a startled cry, she sat up straight in the chair, feet properly on the floor and her hands folded into her lap.

Her mysterious host laughed, the sound like the silver tinkle of bells. "Do not stand on ceremony, Aisling Starchild. You are welcome to make yourself comfortable."

At the sound of her full name, Aisling cocked her head and looked more closely at the magistrate. None but the Fae knew the descriptive that all hatchlings were given on their fiftieth name-day. Each was individual, setting the named apart—thus Ailill was "Brightwing" and she "Starchild" even though they were halves of the same whole.

Even if the magistrate had somehow overheard her given name, he wouldn't have known the other. It was only used by her family and acquaintances in the barrow.

"Should I know you, sir? You do seem familiar..." She dared not speak the thought uppermost in her head—that her host seemed far more Fae than mortal.

"I have been gone too long," he sighed. "Once, I too had my wings, young one. I left Faerie in search of adventure and found love. I assume you have done the same, or you would not be parading in the streets of a mortal stronghold so readily." He smiled kindly at her. "Might I know his name?"

"Fergal O'Connor, Lord," she whispered, gazing down at the twisted fingers in her lap.

"Ah...a good lad and well worth loving. My Laoise was a cousin to his house. It was more than half a century ago that I left the barrow. I am not surprised you don't remember me. I remember when you and your brother first hatched. Your father was so proud of your mother. Twins are so rare... I held the two of you in the palms of my hands, and you looked up at me with those green eyes...it was like a miracle."

Aisling frowned, struggling to remember. This man must have been important to her house, and she could not...

"Do not strain to remember, child. It is part of the price we pay. When we give up our wings, we give up our Fae identities. No one from the barrow will remember you existed. You will know all, but they will be lost to you. Even Ailill will forget your face, I fear...though with the strength of bond between you, perhaps you will be spared that final blow. Do you still wish to pay the price?"

Her heart pounded in her chest. To lose her family, and especially Ailill, was a hard price to pay. Fergal's face rose up before her mind's eye. It was worth it for what she gained.

"Aye, my Lord. I regret Ailill and I parted with harsh words, but that is as may be. My future lies with Fergal O'Connor, and so lies the way of it."

"You know what you must do?"

"I must go seek the White Lady, Rhiannon. Only she can grant my boon."

"Even so, lass. And she is a great and terrible queen. She is not easily persuaded, and the cost is sure to be high. Are you prepared to pay it?"

"Whatever she asks."

"Are you so sure?" The magistrate rose and began to pace his sanctuary, his hands clasped behind his back. "I too was young when I went to see the Lady. Young and very much in love. Laoise was the most beautiful creature I had ever seen. I wanted to be with her so badly...I begged Rhiannon on bended knee to grant my petition." He paused and studied her with hooded eyes.

"She looked at me with those cold, terrible eyes and laughed. 'Little fool,' she said. 'Will you give me your wings for my trophy wall? Very well. Here is my price. I will grant your boon, but if ere the one you love fills with child, the child shall come to me.' I agreed, unsure if such a thing would even be possible between mortal and Fae—wings or not."

Aisling sat still. She could sense how hard this was for the man to say but knew she must know all before she faced the Lady herself.

"Ten years passed in a heartbeat. I was still young and virile; Laoise a healthy young woman who loved me with all her soul. When she quickened with child, I remembered the Lady's words, but kept the promise to myself, hoping against hope the Lady had forgotten me and mine." He heaved a ragged sigh before visibly gathering himself together and continuing.

"The babe was delivered in time, a beautiful boy child. His mother held him in her arms, and the light of the stars was in her eyes. She was so proud and happy.

One night, as she suckled our Rioghan at her breast, there was a knock upon the door. I opened it without a second thought, and there stood the White Lady, proud and terrible. She spoke not a word, simply came into the room and lifted the babe from his mother's lap. Laoise protested, and the Lady looked to me. 'Ask Tadhg why I've come,' she said, and then swept out again with the babe in her arms."

Aisling could see the shine of tears in his eyes as he wandered through his memories. She held still and listened. It was all she could do for him.

"Of course, Laoise did as bid. She asked me what had just happened. I tried to explain—but she went mad with grief. Within a fortnight, she was dead by her own hand."

Aisling gasped.

The magistrate turned to her with a sad smile. "It was many years ago now. I have been alone ever since, gradually aging, though not as quickly as my mortal friends. Soon, I will join my Laoise... If you go through with this folly, my dear, make sure you keep nothing from Fergal. Tell him up front what the price may be, and let him help you decide if you both are willing to pay it."

"I will, my Lord," she answered in a small voice.

"Now, you ran off and left him, didn't you? Thinking to come back a mortal and save him the rigors of the journey to the Lady. Something like that?"

"Seamus said—"

"Ah, Seamus." Tadhg nodded. "That explains a lot. He shelters the lad much since his parents died when he was a mere boy."

"He said I must go alone. To protect Fergal from the Unseelie Court. I could no' bear to have him hurt."

"Do you think 'tis wise, starting out with secrecy between you? Should it not be his choice rather than yours?"

"You are right, my Lord. I will go to him and let him choose."

"In the larger scheme of things, 'twill be best, lass. He is a grown man. It is only fair to give him the chance to show his mettle."

Aisling rose to her feet and crossed to the magistrate. She stood on her tiptoes and planted a kiss on the old man's cheek. "Thank you, Lord, for your wise council."

His cheeks flushed a faint rose. "Thank you, my dear. For reminding me what it is to love. I had begun to lose sight of it." He looked down at her speculatively. "Wait here a moment. I have something for you."

Tadhg left the room, and Aisling moved slowly through it, her hand touching the smooth polished wood of the furniture. She breathed in the perfume of autumn roses filling a glass basin. The sound of birds filtered through the open window. It was almost like being in a Faerie glade. He must miss it a great deal, even after all this time. Was she doing the right thing? Fergal's face rose into her mind once again, and she knew she was. Her future was with him.

Tadhg stepped into the room, a cloak thrown over his arm. He shook it out and held it up. "Come here, my dear."

Aisling obeyed.

He slipped the cloak over her shoulders, taking care with her wings. It hung in graceful folds to her feet.

"I thought as much," he nodded. "You and my Laoise were of a size. Take this gift from me. It will hide your true nature from all but the most observant. It will aid you on your journey through mortal lands."

"Thank you again, sir," she murmured. "I realize how much this must mean to you." She fingered the soft velvet of the cloak.

"She needs it no more, child, and would be pleased it was come to good use."

"How can I ever repay you?"

"Be safe. Keep your wits about you when you speak to the Lady. Do not make the same mistake I made."

"I promise to be careful."

"Think of me sometimes when the way is hard. Come to me and speak of Faerie when you need a friend."

"I will." She dropped him a curtsey. "I will remember all you've said."

"Go now, and find your Fergal."

Her heart fluttered at the sound of his name.

Raising the hood of the cloak to shadow her features, she slipped out of the house and into the morning.

* * *

Fergal was frantic. He had been searching for an hour, and the town was not so large she could have disappeared into it. Where could she have gone?

Damn Seamus for a fool! What had he said to the girl to drive her away?

He stopped by his market stall to gather some tools and supplies that would ease the journey she was bound to make.

"Fergal O'Connor!" cried the woman across the way. "Have you heard the latest?"

"What might that be, Molly?" He tried to be polite, but Molly McShane was one of the biggest gossips in the county.

"Lorcan O'Hanlon caught a Fae witch trying to steal the soul of his newborn calf!" She shuddered in vicarious delight. "He said the wicked creature was nose to nose with the wee thing sucking the life out of it."

Fergal froze. "What did he do with her—it?" he asked.

Molly's eyes narrowed, and then she shrugged. "He said he took it to the magistrate for trial. Was promised twenty crowns, he was. Good riddance to vile rubbish, I say. The magistrate will set things right. Just you wait and see."

"What did the creature look like?"

"Lorcan said it were the image of a young girl with green eyes like saucers and hair like flowing blood. She hissed at him and spat a curse in a foreign tongue.

Feared for his life he was! The magistrate was so grateful; he told Lorcan he would soon become a town elder. Imagine!"

For the life of him, Fergal could *not* imagine it. Lorcan O'Hanlon was one of the town wastrels and a mean drunk besides. The magistrate would never credit him with a position of power. But, while the charges were obvious falsehoods, the description was too close to Aisling not to pay it mind. "Good day to you, Molly. Give Lorcan my congratulations when next you meet."

"Where are you going so fast, Fergal? Come in for a spot o' tea."

"No thank you, Molly. I must be off. I-I promised the magistrate I would run an errand for him this morn."

"Well, see if you can get a glimpse of the witch. I wish I had seen her. The Fae are such wicked creatures. It would be a sight to tell the bairns about..."

Fergal waved absently, inwardly seething. *Pompous old cow!*

He hurried toward the magistrate's stately abode, not watching where he was going. He nearly ran down a slim young woman in a velvet cloak and put out a hand to steady her.

"I'm sorry, my Lady. I was no' watching my feet. I am in a hurry—"

"'Tis quite all right, good sir. I've been warned you are out of your head of late." She smiled at him, and he gathered her into his arms.

His heart skipped a beat at the sight of her. "Aisling, love! I thought I had lost you! Why did you leave me sleeping?"

"I was no' thinking clearly, Fergal. But now, I know whatever must be done, we must do together. Will you come with me to the Unseelie Court?"

"I would come with you to the gates of the damned, beloved. You need only ask."

"Where we go is very close to those gates. The White Lady Rhiannon is Queen of Demons and a terrible force indeed."

"If I am at your side, I will be content."

"No matter what the cost?"

He felt his heart skip another beat. "No matter the cost."

Chapter Ten

Ailill slumped down upon the bank of the lake some distance from the castle. He dipped a handful of the icy water in his hand and drank, wincing at the contact with his split lip.

What was he to do now? If he could just get in to see the Dagda, he was sure he could convince Avallach to gift him an apple. But if he couldn't get past the guard, what was he to do?

"You look as though you lost your only friend," came a cheerful voice at his elbow. "Want to talk about it?"

Ailill jumped. He had not seen the fisherman when he sat down, so hidden was the other by reeds. He glanced at the speaker.

The man must be ancient, even by Fae standards. A long beard cascaded down his chest like white-water rapids. His face was a mask of wrinkles, but his eyes twinkled merrily from their places deep inside the caverns. The hands on the fishing pole were gnarled and spotted, and his back was stooped.

"I doubt you can help me, old one," Ailill sighed.

"You might be surprised, hatchling. Tell me your tale."

"Unless you hold the ear of the Dagda, 'tis no use... but it is a simple tale and soon told. I went to the mortal Faire yesterday morn. I know 'tis discouraged, but I grew restless in the barrow and was looking for a bit of a lark." He kept Aisling's name out of his narrative. "While I was strolling the marketplace, I met a girl."

"A mortal girl?"

"Aye but as beautiful as the sun. And as sweet as clover honey. Her heart is brave and true, and I gave her mine to nurture."

"You fell in love."

"Isn't that what I just said?"

The old man's face worked as he fought to suppress a smile. "Go on."

"I came here to see my kinsman the Dagda and crave an apple of immortality for my beloved—"

The old man cut in. "Are you mad, boy? 'Tis no light trinket you would beg. The apple tree bears but once a decade and then only a handful of fruit. These are kept for those wounded in battle or otherwise at risk. To give such a precious thing to a mortal you believe you fancy—"

"I love her with all my heart! I wish to spend the rest of eternity at her side. Is that so difficult to understand? Were you never in love, old one?"

"Aye. To my cost. And married these five centuries to another despite it. The dreams of youth often fall by the wayside with the wisdom of age. What if you change your mind next month, or next year, or next millennia? Would it be fair to the lass who will have lost all she knows by then?"

"I will never change my mind. I love her."

"You met her yester morn. How can you know if you love her?"

"My soul is on fire with her. I would slay a thousand dragons for her smile. I would dare any quest for her favor. I cannot imagine life without her at my side."

"Sounds like love full well. What makes you think the Dagda will help you?"

"He is the King. If he will no' help, who can?"

"True enough, but why should he?"

"For the love he bears my mother, his cousin. For the strength of my father's arm and my brother's service."

"All of those are very well, but they do not tell why he should make an exception to the law for you. What can *you* offer the King to make it worth his while?"

Ailill's heart sank to his toes. "I have nothing to offer. My father has disowned me, and my mother has naught to give. I will set up housekeeping with only my love, but 'twill be enough with Caoimhe at my side."

"You seem a good lad, if a little headstrong. Mayhap I shall grant your boon." He rose to his feet.

"What nonsense are you speaking, old one?" Ailill scoffed. "Only Avallach can grant my boon."

The old man's posture straightened, and his voice deepened. "Then 'tis a good thing I am Avallach." The years seemed to fall away from his face and he smiled at Ailill's gasp. "Do you think I would get much fishing done if I sallied forth myself? Come, lad." He reached a hand down to Ailill. "Let us go and find your lady love."

Ailill gawked at the man before him. "B-but..."

"Close your mouth, Ailill Brightwing. I knew your quest before you spoke. Did not your father rant at me for an hour this morn? But I believe in love. I never got to pursue my dreams. I would be happy to grant you yours."

Ailill scrambled to his feet, bowing low. "My Lord King, how can I repay you?"

"We will discuss the matter anon. For now, I think we should rescue your damsel in distress. My dungeons can be cold and lonely."

He strode forward, and Ailill had to hurry to catch up. He was breathless by the time they reached the guardhouse.

The surly sentry who had stopped the lovers earlier stepped into his path. "Where do you think you are going, whelp? I told you—"

"What did you tell him, Ruarc?" asked Avallach, coming forward. "I would very much like to know what kept my kinsman cooling his heels at my gate when he came to speak to me."

Ruarc's face paled. "My Lord," he murmured, bowing low. "I was only following orders."

"So you were. Now, you have new orders. Ailill Brightwing is free to come and go within my castle as he pleases. Do you understand?"

"Yes, my Lord."

Ailill could smell the stench of fear rising off the other. It made his heart sing.

"Where is the young mortal who accompanied my cousin hither?"

"S-she is in the dungeon, my Lord King."

"Go and fetch her to the throne room. I must change."

"As you command, sire." The guard bowed low once more, but Ailill saw the hatred in his eyes. Here was a man who hated being reprimanded and made a fool. He was a dangerous ally and would be an implacable enemy. Ailill resolved to be on his guard around the other.

"Well, what are you waiting for?" asked Avallach impatiently. "I wish to speak to the girl immediately. Do not dally longer, or you shall take her place below! Come along, Ailill."

He turned and moved toward the castle, not bothering to look back.

Ailill hurried to catch up to him, casting an uneasy glance over his shoulder to the glowering guardsman. "My King," he began nervously, "was that wise?"

"Ruarc is my finest captain," replied Avallach. "I trust him implicitly. He will bring your lady to you."

Ailill hoped the King was right, but he feared the hatred in the other's eyes.

As they strode on through the castle, Ailill looked around him with undisguised delight. The palace was the pinnacle of Faerie architecture. The crystal walls were so clear the outdoors seemed separated from them by nothing more than distance. There was no need for painting or tapestry as decoration. Nothing could compare to the beauty without. The floor beneath their feet was black marble with thin veins and swirls of gold. It was like looking into the night sky. Above them, the ceiling rose in dizzying swoops supported by beams of crystal bound with gold.

The furnishings were all gilded wood with thick green cushions. Ailill wanted to sink down into one of those chairs and let his weariness fall away, but there was no rest to be had as Avallach hurried through his domain.

At last, he stopped before a gilded door. "Here is the throne room," he said, throwing open the door. "Sit you down and rest. I shall return soon, and we will sort out this affair."

"Thank you, my King," Ailill replied with a low bow.

Avallach continued on his way, and Ailill stepped into the opulent chamber. Here the cushions were of crimson, trimmed in gold. He sank down gratefully on a petitioner's chair, trying to still his whirling thoughts.

The King would grant his plea. He had not thought far beyond this point. What would they do once Caoimhe ate of the apple and they had an eternity before them? They could not go back to the aerie, but it was dangerous to live far from the city. There was the Unseelie Court to contend with. Without the protection of the crystal castle, life was a constant struggle...

He thought of Caoimhe's golden hair and flawless skin. He remembered how she made him laugh and how her smile lit his world. Somehow, they would survive.

* * *

Caoimhe huddled in the corner of the lightless cell she had been thrown into. Here there was no crystal clarity but only granite gray walls and dank dampness. The only concession to creature comforts in the cell was a pile of moldy straw in the opposite corner, but when she neared it, she heard scrabbling in the straw that spoke of bugs or vermin, and she backed away. *I suppose I will be beyond caring soon enough.* For now, however, she would stay away.

She had measured the cell in careful paces, feeling her way along the wall. It was twenty paces wide, and fifteen long. Bigger than her tiny room at home but 'twas no comfort. At home, she had a window to watch the stars and a goose-down mattress to soften her bed.

At home, she was cosseted and made much of. She was an only child and came late to her mother's loins. All her life, she had been the spoiled darling. A rude awakening this—to find herself in an alien prison. She felt her lip begin to tremble and fought back the tears. She would be strong! Ailill had promised to save her. He would keep his word.

If only they had left a light. It would be so much better if she could see what she faced rather than merely hear the skittering across the stone floor. Her imagination was getting the better of her, and she would go mad if left in the dark for long. Already the cell was peopled with hulking ghosts and leering demons summoned by her imagination.

Where was Ailill? Was he safe? She had seen him fall to the ground after the guard's blow. Though he regained his feet, was he hurt? Had the guards let him be after she was gone?

She felt a tear slide past her guard to travel down her cheek and plop onto her skirt. Why had she come?

Aye, the Fae was a handsome devil...but she had forsaken hearth and home for him on an hour's acquaintance. Was she mad? Logic said so. To fancy herself in love—and with a Fae—after so short a time together she must be.

Why then did she feel as if her world would end without him? Why was she ready to give up her mortal life to live forever among the Fae if only he was by her side?

She hid her face in her hands and let the sobs come. She missed her mother. She missed the brindle cat. Were there cats in Faerie? What was she to do?

There was the scrape of a key in the lock, and Caoimhe shrank back against the wall. Her captors had whispered there was only one circumstance that would set her free—death. She did not want to die. She had a youthful perspective on life and fancied herself living into the far-flung reaches of time.

The door swung open, and the light of a torch hurt her eyes. She held a hand before her face, squinting in the bright light.

"Come with me, mortal." Disgust colored the order. "I am to take you before the King."

Chapter Eleven

Aisling and Fergal walked in silence, fingers entwined. They could think of little to say at first, but as the day wore on, confidences spilled forth.

"There are six of us offspring in my family," she told him, "my brother Darragh is eldest, then Ailill and I. Twins are a rare gift among the Fae. One in a thousand births, and any birth is uncommon enough. The Fae do no' normally have large families. Only because we are related to the royal house are there so many of us, I think."

"You said there were six of you?"

"Yes, the next after us is my sister Sorcha, then Tanai, and last the baby Easnadh." "Sounds like a lively bunch."

She smiled a little sadly. "Aye. It was never dull."

"You will miss your family."

"Mayhaps. But my place is now with you."

He squeezed her hand, and a thrill of happiness ran through her. She could not believe her fortune. It would be worth any cost. She only regretted she could not share her happiness with her mother.

"My family is smaller than yours," Fergal told her. "You've met the whole lot of us. Seamus is all I have left. My parents were taken by fever when I was a mere babe, and he raised me from the first. What a trial I was to a middle-aged widower...but somehow he managed it."

"I'd say he managed it quite well," she teased, with a fond smile.

"I thank you, lady, but I fear you may be biased."

They laughed together, easy in their companionship.

The day wore on, the sun climbing higher in the sky, and the cloak Tadhg had given her hung heavy on her shoulders. She wished she could remove it, but 'twould not do to walk the mortal lands with wings exposed. She realized now the risk she had taken at the Faire, and it sent a shiver down her spine.

"Are you well, beloved?" asked Fergal anxiously.

She smiled weakly at him. "Aye. I was merely thinking."

He brushed a tendril of copper curl from her forehead. "Do no' worry, love. It will all be well."

"I hope you are right, but I am sore afraid. You do no' know the Unseelie Court, Fergal. It is a terrible place filled with vile, wicked creatures who hate the Seelie Sidhe. My mother is cousin to the Dagda, the King of the Seelie Court. I do no' know what reception can come from the White Lady. But I fear her wrath."

"I will be at your side, Aisling. I will protect you."

"If only it were so easy..." She sighed.

They had left the village far behind now, and the moor through which they traveled was dotted with fens, which released noxious gases into the heated air. The resultant miasma was visible in low clouds and streams of mist that burned the throat as they struggled through them. Swarms of insects buzzed around their heads and sought to invade any opening they could reach.

Fergal helped Aisling over the uneven ground as her skirts grew heavier and heavier, soaking up the fetid water of the bogs. The effort of slogging through the marsh was wearing on her.

At last, she sank onto the ground, unable to go any further. "I can't," she panted. "I must rest."

Fergal eyed the sky. "'Tis almost sunset. Shall I try to light a fire?"

"No!" she cried, clutching at his arm. "We must no' draw their attention. 'Tis more than our lives are worth to meet the Unseelie band after the sun goes down."

She drew the velvet cloak around her, huddling in its relative warmth. She shivered uncontrollably at the thought of the Lady's Court.

Fergal sank down beside her and slipped his arm around her slim shoulders, taking care not to crush her wings. He rested his chin on her bent head. "Tell me about them, Aisling. I should know what we face. 'Tis only right."

She shuddered. "The Unseelie Court lies in the shadows of Dunnough Tor. The dark barrow mimics the Faerie realm of the Seelie, but all is twisted. Unnatural creatures borne of wicked pairings inhabit the Dark Kingdom. The darker Fae, bogies and goblin redcaps, nuckelavees with their horse's body and skinless arms, banshees, all haunt that realm. Cruelest of all is the Dark Host who ride the Wild Hunt and snatch the unwary traveler to swell their ranks. Over all this madness rules the White Lady, fair Rhiannon, as terrible as she is beautiful. She alone can grant my plea and make me mortal. But she is no' easily swayed."

Fergal drew her head down to rest upon his lap. "Sleep now, Aisling. The world will seem much clearer in the sunlight."

"Aye," she whispered, wracked by shudders. "The night is no time to speak of such horrors." Calmed by his words, she let her eyes drift shut and was soon fast asleep.

"Sleep, beloved," Fergal whispered. "I will watch over you."

* * *

Fergal spread her cloak around them both, resolved to watch through the night. Soon enough, however, the day's exertions caught up with him, and his chin nodded to his chest.

A sudden snap of dried twig brought him instantly awake, staring intently into the darkness, but he could see nothing—save in the distance the faintest glimmer. Could it be red eyes glaring at him? It was enough to dispel all desire to sleep.

His nerves jangled in the moonless dark. Only a dull hint of star-shine broke through the veil of clouds. He was used to house and hearth, not vagabond ways. What was he doing here? What madness had brought him?

Aisling stirred, moaning softly in her sleep, and his arm tightened about her. Here was his purpose—this Fae maid, willing to give her immortality to stand at his side. No greater gift graced this world.

The night was chill, and he shivered, drawing the velvet cloak more closely about his shoulders, and tucking it in about Aisling. His hand lingered on her shoulder. She was so fragile, so delicate. He wanted only to protect her, come what may.

"Man..."

The voice seemed a trick of his imagination. Merely a whisper on the wind. He paid it no mind.

"Man..." This time the word was a little louder, as if the speaker were closer.

"Who is there?" he challenged hoarsely, his heart in his throat.

"What do ye here upon my moor, man? Why come ye hither in the cold night?"

Fergal felt his pulse pounding in his temples and fought to keep his voice steady. "I was on my way to Dunan town and misjudged the path. I ask no more than peace till morn, and I will be traveling on."

"Man...I smell Fae upon ye. Which Court do ye serve?" There was a shuffling sound, and Fergal caught a glimpse of movement. His interrogator was slipping closer.

"I-I serve no Court, Lord. I am no' worthy."

The sound of a rusty chuckle filled the darkness, and again the creature shuffled closer. "Shall I aid ye on thy way, man? I will for a ha'penny. No one knows the moor better than Black Tom."

Fergal could see the stooped shape in the starlight now. The creature was no more than a yard away. He swallowed hard, fighting down his panic. He must keep his wits if he hoped to best one of the marsh men. "Thank ye kindly for your offer, Lord, but I am sure now of the way and will be about it come the dawn."

Black Tom stepped a little closer. Now that Fergal's eyes were used to the starlight, he could see the wizened old creature. It looked like a short man, with straggly hair and a long-tailed cap. Black Tom looked at Aisling, still sleeping soundly. His long thin nose sniffed the air. "What hast ye there, man? A Faerie maid ye has captured for yer own? Best be ware—her sort are fickle as the wind in autumn. Ye were well to be rid of her. If 'tis a Fae bride ye seek, I can set you on the path to a finer one."

"Thank ye again, Master Tom, but no. I am quite content with my Lady."

"And who might your lady be?" asked the other. "Not many Seelie Sidhe here on Dead Dog Moor."

"My name is mine to give or hold," said Aisling before Fergal had a chance to answer. She sat up abruptly, her hand curled into a ball. "Get ye gone, piskie, before I singe your coat tails." Within her cupped fingers began a kernel of rapidly brightening light. "Ye know what I can do. Get ye gone!"

In the unnatural light radiating from her hand, Fergal could see her eyes were narrowed into slits and her face harsh with an expression of pure hatred. He had never seen this side of her. It sent a chill through him.

Black Tom whined, "Come now, Lady. I meant no disrespect. I wished to pay homage to a fair Sidhe. Tom is a faithful servant to the Seelie Court."

The light leaking from between her fingers was now so bright Fergal had to shield his eyes.

"You dare to lie to me? Get ye gone, foul fiend, lest ye feel my wrath!" Aisling rose to her knees and drew her hand back as if to throw the ball of light.

"I go. I go!" Black Tom wailed, scampering off into the darkness. "My mistress shall know of this. Ye shall see. When the Lady knows...then ye shall see!"

Aisling sighed, and the ball of fire dissipated. She slumped against him.

"What was that?" he asked her.

"A piskie. One of the minor creatures of Rhiannon's Court. The piskies love to lead travelers astray. Follow a piskie, and you may well find yourself facedown in a bog till the end of time."

He took the hand that had held the light in his. "And what was this?" he asked gravely.

"A wee bit of Faerie magic. More to scare than harm, though it might well have stung his backside a bit were I to have loosed it."

"What other secrets have you held from me, Aisling?"

"What do you mean?" she asked, her tone evasive.

"You did no' tell me you had the power to make light from darkness. What else can you do?"

"Little magics. Nothing of importance."

"What else?" he insisted.

"I can hasten growth in seedlings and sometimes bring the rain...I can raise a breeze in a still sky and sew the moonbeams into cloth. What does it matter? If Rhiannon grants my boon, all the magic will be gone."

"No."

"W-what do you mean, 'no'?"

"It is too much to give up, Aisling. I cannot let you do it."

"It is my choice, Fergal O'Connor. I freely make it."

"You never told me you had such gifts. 'Twas bad enough you wished to lose eternity. I cannot take so much from you."

"You cannot stop me!"

"But I do no' have to aid you either. If you wish to go through with this madness, to give up all you possess, it is up to you. But do no' do it for my sake. I will no be a part of it." He rose to his feet, trembling like a leaf. "I cannot."

He stumbled into the darkness. Her magic was strong enough she had no need of him. Come the dawn, she would see her folly. She could still return home to those who loved her.

"Fergal!" she cried out behind him, the anguish in her voice almost giving him pause.

No, he must save her from herself. He stumbled onward, feeling his way in the darkness.

He passed within a handbreadth of Black Tom who smiled secretively to himself, repeating the names Aisling and Fergal O'Connor until he had them burned into his memory.

Chapter Twelve

Caoimhe stood, painfully conscious of her rumpled skirts and disheveled hair. *One look, and the King will send me packing. Or worse, order me executed rather than release me from Faerie.* She could feel the tears starting up the back of her throat and coughed to mask it.

I will no' cry! she swore to herself. *No matter what may come.*

The liveried guard at the door growled, "Get a move on, human. The King is a busy man. He does no' have all day to wait on your whim."

Caoimhe staggered forward, her legs cramped from her hours of confinement. Or was it days? She had no way to tell. Everything seemed confused in her head.

The guard pushed her roughly as she passed him, sending her stumbling. She fought to keep her balance but fell against the rough stone wall of the hallway, scraping her hands and cheek as she tried to catch herself.

The Fae grabbed her arm and pulled her after him. She had to trot to keep up. Her heart was pounding in her chest. What would become of her?

They hurried through twisting corridors and up stone stairways. The journey was a confused blur of glass walls and distant scenery. The furnishings were gilded wood, and under different circumstances, she would have stood and admired the workmanship—but there was no time to catch her breath, much less study the furniture.

She banged her feet painfully against the granite risers as the guard dragged her along. By the time he paused before a closed doorway, her toes were bloody and bruised. She wanted to weep, such was her desperation, but she had promised herself, and she forced herself to be strong.

The guard straightened his emerald tunic and drew himself up tall. He opened the door and shoved her through it.

Caoimhe fell through the open doorway onto thick crimson carpeting that gave beneath her scraped hands. Her knees jarred until her teeth clicked together. At least the blood won't show, she thought with a silent giggle of hysteria.

She heard a wordless cry of alarm and felt arms go around her shoulders. "Come, beloved, let me help you to a chair."

"Ailill," she whispered. "Is it you?" She collapsed against him, holding to him with all her might. He felt so...solid after all her solitary imaginings. "I was so frightened."

"My poor child," came a soft, deep voice from in front of her, "please, come forward."

Ailill helped her to her feet, his arm securely around her waist. She limped forward, reveling in the comfort of his support.

He led her to a soft chair and helped her into it, hovering behind the chair.

"You are a pretty little thing," murmured the same voice, and she looked up.

Sitting before her on a high-backed gilt throne was a male Fae with a long white beard and a golden circlet upon his brow. His clothing was simple in style, yet rich in fabric—a russet doublet of velvet worn over dark green leggings with knee high boots. Power radiated from him without any outward manifestation beyond the simple crown.

This then was the Dagda. Her heart climbed into her throat, and she went down on one knee before her chair. "Your Majesty," she whispered.

"Rise, child. Sit. You are tired and have been used cruelly." His face tightened, and he turned to the guard who remained standing beside the door. "Tell Ruarc I am most displeased. We shall speak of it later."

The guard blanched. "Yes, my Lord." He beat a hasty retreat.

Ailill helped Caoimhe to her feet and settled her back into her chair. "All will be well, beloved. He has given his consent," he whispered in her ear.

Caoimhe's heart soared. It hadn't been for naught. All would be well.

"Now, my child," murmured Avallach, "tell me...are you ready to spend eternity among the Fae? 'Twill not be an easy thing. You will not be able to change your mind. The people you know and love in the mortal realm will wither and die, and you will go on. Look at me, child. How many years would you say I had walked this earth?"

She knew it was a test. The Dagda was not mortal, so despite the fact he appeared no older than her elderly father, she knew he must be much older. "Twenty score?" she guessed timidly.

Avallach laughed delightedly. "Well done, lady. You do not flatter. But you are far from the mark. I am twenty times as much. I was old when this land was new. Your swain here is more than a quarter the number you guessed. Can you love so ancient a creature? He was a stripling when your great-grandfather was born."

Caoimhe felt her head spin. "I love him, my Lord," she whispered. "I would give him whatever he wished."

The Dagda nodded. He shifted in his gilded throne, throwing one leg over the arm of the chair and swinging his foot. "'Tis well," he answered distractedly. "He has asked me for a boon, a favor for you. He wishes to grant you immortality. Such a gift must carry a price. Are you ready to pay it?"

"What must I do, lord?" Her heart climbed once more to her throat, and instinctively, she clutched Ailill's hand.

"We will speak of it after you have rested." He rose from his throne and crossed the thick carpet to the massive fireplace. A huge cauldron hung upon a hook over the crackling fire, savory steam rising from it to perfume the air with the scent of stew.

Taking a dipper from its place on the hearth, he dipped it into the cauldron and filled a golden bowl. He brought it to where she sat and handed it to her. "You must be hungry, my dear. Eat. There is plenty more." He gestured toward the fire. "This is my second greatest treasure, the inexhaustible cauldron. With it, I can feed my entire Court."

Her mouth dropped open in wonder. "Truly, lord? 'Tis a marvel indeed."

"Eat," he urged.

She had never tasted anything as delicious. The stew seemed to melt in her mouth. "'Tis wonderful," she sighed. "Such a feast would raise the saddest heart and fill the richest belly."

"Merely one of the secrets of the Fae." His face creased in a frown. "Such secrets cannot be whispered in the mortal world. They would come in force and try to destroy Faerie. That is why you can never go back. You have only one choice, Caoimhe Sinclair. Stay as Ailill's bride, or stay as a guest of my dungeon. I doubt the choice will be difficult."

"Nay, my Lord. He is my life." She felt Ailill's hand tighten on her shoulder.

"As I thought. Now we must speak of the price," murmured Avallach.

* * *

Ailill's hand tightened on Caoimhe's shoulder. Now was the moment. The Dagda had already told Ailill he would exact a great price for the golden apple. He had pledged to pay his part of it whatever it might be, though he did not foresee how they could accomplish any quest weaponless and without aid. It was sure to be a dread cost, and he feared it would frighten her cruelly.

Ailill heard Caoimhe's indrawn breath. "Name it, and I shall pay," she murmured, her voice a mere thread of sound.

He wanted to shout, "Be careful, beloved. The Fae are fickle creatures, and cruel..." but he held his tongue. What would the Dagda ask? It was sure to be difficult at best, perhaps impossible. What would they do if it were unattainable? He would not leave her. Even if it meant his wings.

"I have need of someone to perform a task," continued the Dagda, returning to his throne. "If you complete it, I will give you the golden apple you seek."

"What is your task, Lord?" asked Ailill, wary of the cost.

"I was...less than discreet in a liaison I got caught up in recently. Somehow, I lost a very powerful item in a game of chance with the lady in question. I cannot simply go and ask for the item back myself. It would be awkward at best and tragic at worst."

"What is it you have lost, Sire?"

Avallach bowed his head and studied his clasped hands. "I lost my greatest treasure, the harp Uaithne, in a wager with the Morrigan. I am sure you can see the consequences, cousin, even if your Lady does not."

Aye, he knew. If the Dagda did not play in the change of seasons, the sun forgot its tasks. It would rise and set, but there would be no winter to nurture the sleeping seedlings. There would be no spring to see them born—no summer's heady perfume. It would be one continuous gray day after another, with no other end in sight.

"If I do not get the harp back in time to turn the seasons, there will be terror and heartache throughout both Kingdoms. Already the weather turns unseasonable. Only by convincing the lady to return my instrument may I fulfill my obligation to the world. 'Tis one week's time until the season slips from summer to autumn. Bring me my harp before that day, and you shall get your wish."

Ailill's heart stood still until he reminded it to beat. The Morrigan could be a wicked, vengeful goddess when she wished to be—for all she had ever been kind to him. Getting her to give up so marvelous a prize would be like holding back the moon's flight.

"As you say," he murmured dully, "so let it be done."

"I do not envy you the trying, lad. The Morrigan can be a shrew at best. 'Twas foolish of me to wager Uaithne, but I have done so, and the lady in question has taken possession of the instrument. I asked her to reconsider our wager, and let me replace the harp with precious stones and gold, but she claims to have a fancy for it and will not relent."

"What can we do, Lord?"

The Dagda stood, tugging his tunic into place with the unconscious fastidiousness of the vain. "Beard the lioness in her den. Go to her tower and crave she return it to you. It is your own decision how you go about the winning of it. Bring me Uaithne safe and sound, and I will give you what you require."

So saying, he stepped from the dais and gestured toward the door, as if inviting them to leave.

Ailill helped Caoimhe to her feet. There was nothing more to say. They had been given an impossible task, and if they failed, both their worlds would be at stake.

CHAPTER THIRTEEN

Fergal stumbled onward in the darkness, barely able to make out his hand before his face. The incident with Black Tom played over and over in his mind. Who would have thought Aisling had such powers? He had never even suspected such gifts. Was he wrong to leave her? A dozen times he started to turn around and return, but he stayed his course and continued onward.

She was better off without him. Come the dawn, she would return to the land of the Sidhe, and he would find his way back home. Seamus was right. He should have listened...

A keen wind began to blow, chilling him to the bone. He shivered. There were voices on the wind, and he found himself staring off into the darkness around him. Was that a movement to his left?

"Is there someone there?" he cried out. "Answer me!"

"No one here," the wind whispered, and a cackle of laughter cut off abruptly.

Fergal bent and felt for a rock or stick—anything with which he could defend himself. He cut his hand on the wiry marsh grasses, but there was nothing else in reach.

A howl filled the night, raising the hairs on his neck. It sounded as if all the hounds of hell were circling him where he stood. "I'm no' afraid!" he shouted.

"You should be," came the retort, in a deep voice that chilled his blood.

He spun around. The voice had come from behind

him, but there was no one there. "Show yourself!" he ordered.

"I do not think you would be pleased, man-child," boomed the voice. Now it came from in front of him.

He was being circled, played with. The thought made him angry. "I am no callow boy! Show yourself. I will no' be toyed with!"

A shadow moved to the left of him, and Fergal spun to face it. The creature hulked like a darker gray mountain against the faint star-shine. There was a rattle and click coming from it as it stepped closer.

Suddenly Fergal very much did not wish to see what was approaching. He backed away, but it came ever closer, slow and deliberate, eating the ground with its strides.

Fergal stepped off the path in his retreat, and cold water rose inside his boots. He felt something slither around his ankle and felt a tug.

Crying out in horrified disgust, he tried to jerk his foot free.

There was a bubbling gurgle from the muddy water at his feet, and he saw the shine of eyes below him. Long bony fingers circled his ankle, and he could not break free of their grip.

The hulking shape was drawing closer, and he distinctly heard the clank of chains. He had been raised on the tales of the marshes, and he knew what fit the description—a huge creature girdled in chains could only be Jack-in-Irons, with his killing club and belt of heads ripped mid-scream from the bodies of his victims.

Fergal felt his heart pounding in his chest as he reached down and tore at the bony fingers clutching his foot. He could see a face now, beneath the water, grinning at him with a mouth overfull of pointed teeth.

The water hag jerked his foot out from under him, with a gurgling cackle.

Fergal pin-wheeled his arms, desperately fighting for balance. He lost the fight and tumbled onto his back in the shallow pool. It rose above his head before he could get a decent breath, and he opened his mouth to scream before he thought. Fetid marsh water poured down his throat, and he gagged. His arms flailed for purchase. He had to get out!

A huge hand closed about the front of his jerkin and lifted him from the water.

Gasping for breath, Fergal struggled weakly to get free, but he was thrown over the giant's shoulder, head hanging halfway down the creature's back. A smack on the back forced out the water he had swallowed in a retching gush.

"The queen wants this one, Jenny. You best wait for other meat," grated the giant to the water hag screeching at his feet.

Fergal's head was spinning. He let himself hang limp until he realized he was nose to nose with a corpse-less head. He scrabbled against the giant's broad back, desperately trying to wriggle free.

"Hold still, manling," ordered Jack in his boulder-grating growl. "My Lady ordered Jack to bring you to her, and bring you I shall. She wasn't too specific about what condition you should arrive in. I only assumed it should be breathing."

Fergal froze. While there was life, there was hope. Wasn't there?

* * *

Aisling stared after Fergal. Her Fae sight was unimpaired by the darkness. To her, it was clear as daylight...but she did not follow. Her heart was lying in pieces at her feet, and she could not bear to gather them up so quickly.

She huddled into the velvet cloak, taking comfort in its warmth. It was far more than the attributes of the cloth that warmed her—it was the giver as well. Tadhg had renounced Faerie for *his* love, and all had been well... Then she remembered the end of his tale. No, all had *not* been well.

Perhaps mortal and Fae were not meant to fall in love—at best to share a moment's dalliance and then part.

She rested her forehead on her bent knees and let the tears come. Round as pearls, the Faerie tears spilled from her eyes to cascade upon the path. Some country lass mayhap would find them in the dust and string them for beads.

"Not so High-and-Mighty now, is it?" chortled a gleeful voice. "What 'tis wrong, *Aisling*. Has yer mortal gone and left ye? Tsk-tsk."

Her head jerked up. The piskie! And he knew her true name. Damn the folly that had made her give it to Fergal.

"What do you want, you pest?" she snarled. "Have you come to drive home the knife? So be it! Yes. He's gone. Are you happy?"

Black Tom hunkered down beside her, his bright button eyes glittering with malevolence. "Aye. That I am. Threaten me with Faerie fire, would ye? Ye deserve this and more. I should let ye sit and dissolve yerself in tears, I should. If 'twere up to me, 'tis exactly what I would do!"

"Get on with it then. I grow weary of your company."

"'Tain't up to me. I've got me orders, and I don't go against the Lady. 'Tis more than me life would be worth..."

"What are you babbling about?"

"The Lady has sent for ye. I am to take ye to the barrow."

Aisling felt her heart skip. "How did the Lady know I was about the moor?"

"The Lady knows all, fool. Ye'd best get yerself together so's we may get on with it. Be glad ye get me for a guide. Yer Fergal weren't so lucky."

"What do you mean?" She reached out and grabbed the piskie's arm in a vice-like grip. "What do you know of Fergal?"

"Ow! Ye are hurting me! Let ye loose of me!"

She shook his arm. "I'll show you hurting if you don't answer my question, wart!"

"Jack's got him; Tall Jack with the chains and skulls; Jack the Giant, tee hee."

"Blast you, piskie! Jack-in-Irons was sent for Fergal?"

"'Tis what I said. Leave go my arm. Ye will snap the bone, ye will."

"And it will mend ere morn if I do. Best you be ware, or it will be your scrawny neck I twist, and there is no remedy for such as that!"

"Temper, Faerie! Are ye sure ye be Seelie?" His face set in a pout. "I only do what I am told, and ye abuse me for the doing."

Aisling's eyes narrowed. "I swear, piskie, if you do no' tell me all, and quickly too, I shall truly wring your neck!" She shook him until his teeth rattled in his head.

"All right! All right! I'll tell ye all I know!" he squealed.

Aisling let him go, and sat back on her heels, arms folded across her chest. "Get on with it."

"I watched your swain away from here. He went but a little down the road before Jack caught him up. Jenny Greenteeth tried to trap him in the marsh, but Jack would have none of that. He has taken the mortal to the barrow. The Lady sent for both of ye. How she knew ye were about, only the Lady knows, and I ask no questions. She is my Queen, and I do as she say."

Aisling rose to her feet. "Let's go."

"Ah, 'tis another story now, I see! When 'tis yer idea to hurry, hurry I must. Fine! For the sake of the Lady, I will take ye there. 'Tis a long way, though, and Jack will be there long ere ye can wend yer way."

"Then we must get started, mustn't we?"

"Such a hurry," he gloated. "For a mortal who spurned you!"

"Do no' trifle with me. I have had enough of your machinations. 'Tis your tricks that drove Fergal away in the first place."

"Untrue! Untrue! He is like any of the flesh-skinned ones. He saw your power, and he fled like a frightened babe."

Aisling's temper was truly beginning to get away from her. Her fingers began to glow with the Faerie fire. "If he fled because of my powers, 'twould be a shame to waste them, wouldn't it?" She leaned closer to him.

"I could call a mount if ye wish," offered the piskie hastily, backing away from her. "There's an aughisky lives nearby."

"I am no mortal to be tricked so. Will he bear us true?"

"As ye say, ye are no mortal. He has no taste for the flesh of Fae. The pride of the Lady's stables he is." His eyes glittered with glee. "Lucky ye are he does not carry Fergal, for the coast is no' far, and even *I* can smell the sea." His nose twitched as if to prove his claim.

"Call the beast. I do no' wish to keep the Lady waiting. And neither should you if her wrath is as told."

The piskie paled to the color of drowned flesh. "Aye, 'tis true. She is no' to be trifled with."   He put two grimy fingers into his wide mouth and whistled, the sound piercing in the still night air.

Aisling's sharp ears caught a distant whinny and the sound of galloping hooves. A pale shape loomed out of the night, and a fish-gray horse with bulging eyes and blood-red nostrils raced out of the darkness.

She shivered. The aughisky was one of the wicked creatures she had warned Fergal about. The Unseelie Court was full of such abominations. Even the thought of trusting one of them rankled, but there was no choice. They mustn't leave Fergal in the Lady's clutches any longer than necessary. He may have abandoned her, but she would not do the same to him. It was for her sake he had ventured to the moor, and she would see him safely home if he still wished to go.

Her heart fell at the thought the whole journey might have been for naught, but she straightened her shoulders and grabbed hold of the aughisky's mane. Fluttering her wings to lift her to the creature's broad back, she slung her leg over. She reached down and grabbed the piskie's hand, jerking it up to sit behind her.

"Which way?"

"Give it its head. It knows the way."

Taking a deep breath, Aisling did as he bid. The Unseelie horse leapt forward, and she clung to the mane with both hands. As the path melted away beneath them, one question rang over and over in her mind. *Would they make it to the Court on time?*

CHAPTER FOURTEEN

The land of the Sidhe was a beautiful place. Everywhere Caoimhe looked there was another breathtaking sight to behold. Here at the eternal cusp of springtime, the grass was a velvet green carpet under her bare feet, soft as baby's hair. Fields of tiny, white star-shaped flowers nodded at them as they passed, perfuming the air with an indefinable fragrance hinting at both roses and wood smoke but close kin to neither. Brilliant blue-plumed birds darted through the cloudless skies, their high, clear calls ringing in the stillness. To Caoimhe, it seemed a paradise. Particularly in contrast to the dungeon of the crystal keep.

As they walked, however, she came to notice that not all was beautiful. Here grew a stunted rosebush, its blossoms edged with black, conspicuous amongst its fellows. There stood a twisted tree, bare branches lifting gnarled fingers to the cloudless sky. She shivered, suddenly chilled.

"What is it, love?" asked Ailill softly.

"Something is wrong here," she answered. "I can't explain it..."

"It will get more intense as we go. The Morrigan is a complex being, she is. But she has ever been good to me. I hope 'twill aid us in the quest, but I do no' pretend it likely to be without cost."

"Tell me about her."

"She is a dark queen. Many call her mad. She is a blood goddess and a harbinger of war. She can be quite beautiful, young and flame-haired...or an ancient crone with a croaking raven on her shoulder. She is a trickster when she wishes to be, but she's always treated me fairly." He sighed. "I don't know what we can offer her that will stir her heart. She is powerful and proud. The Dagda has much history with her as well. She will no' easily be persuaded to do him a good deed."

"Is there then no hope?" Caoimhe felt the tightening in her throat that presaged tears and willed herself not to cry. She would make the best of what she was offered, and if it were merely a lifetime at his side, she would be content.

Ailill stared at the grass beneath their feet as they walked.

It worried her he would not look at her. "Is there something more I should know? Please, Ailill—tell me the worst of it."

"You have crossed the borders of Faerie now, Caoimhe. You have eaten of Fae food. There is no returning to your life as it was before. Once you have tasted the food of Faerie, you are bound here for life. Already the mortal world will have begun to forget you ever existed. But there is no proper place for us in Faerie if we don't succeed. The land itself will no' willingly accept a mortal. It will begin to wilt and die. We have to convince her, or we are both doomed to wander outcasts through a land blighted by the loss of its seasons."

She took a deep breath and let it out in a shuddering rush of air. "What will we do?"

"I don't know. I can't think of anything the Morrigan needs. We have nothing of value to offer. If she can't be won over by the desperation of our plight, then we are done for, and so is the world. I hope I can persuade her how important the seasons be to the mortal realm, but I warn you—there is no love lost between her and mankind either. She is a jealous goddess and has been slighted often enough to hold a grudge."

The land they walked through now bore little resemblance to the lush pastoral landscape surrounding the crystal keep. The trees were bare and twisted into complex patterns of branches above ground and knotted into cat's-cradles of roots below. In places, hillocks seemingly comprised entirely of root systems loomed beside the path, scarlet and golden leaves trapped in the net of their interlaced web. It was beautiful and terrible at once.

The bright blue birds singing in the sky were gone. In their places were cawing ravens that perched in the twisted treetops and peered down at them through intelligent yellow eyes. As they moved down the rocky path, the ravens called down the line, announcing their coming to whomever might hear.

Caoimhe shivered and stepped closer to Ailill. The pathway cut into her tender feet, and she bit back cries of pain. It was a horrible place, and the sun was beginning to sink. Would they be caught out in this wasteland when night fell?

Ailill's arm tightened about her shoulders. "Don't worry, love. It isn't as bad as it seems. We are still in the Sidhe barrow, despite what it may appear. At least we are safe from the Unseelie band here in Faerie."

"The Unseelie?"

"Aye. You've heard me speak of them, haven't you?

They are the dark Fae—the wicked masters of the Wild Hunt. Their Court is a mockery of the Dagda's entourage. But they cannot enter into the Faerie barrow without permission. The worst we face is cold and hunger. We will survive."

She told herself she had to trust him. He wouldn't lie to her...would he? The Dagda's stew was long since worked off by their journey, and she winced to hear her stomach growl its disapproval.

Ailill smiled down at her, fond amusement radiating from his emerald eyes. "I know, love. I could clear an orchard of *driw* single-handedly."

"*Driw*! I had forgotten." She thrust her hand into the pocket of her apron and pulled out the slightly mashed fruit she had stowed on their first day in Faerie.

His eyes lit up. "That's my clever girl! A *driw* will satisfy any hunger, no matter how great. 'Tis why you never need more than one. Even if we share this, it should stave the hunger for the evening at least." He pulled a slim-bladed dagger from his boot and split the fruit in two rough halves, giving her the larger piece.

"No," she protested, "you take the bigger. You need it more than I."

"I am used to the properties of the fruit. Believe me, love, I will be quite content with the smaller half."

Reluctantly, she took what he offered and bit into the purple pulp. The juices ran down her parched throat in a spate of welcome relief. And, as he had promised, by the time she had finished her half of the fruit she was feeling well-satisfied and ready to go on.

"Come, beloved. I know a place where we can shelter for the night. It is no' far from here." He took her hand. "It will give you a chance to rest your feet and let me care for your bruises."

She remembered how he had healed the stone bruise on their first day and nodded. "I am beginning to feel weary," she admitted.

"It is just over that rise," he promised, pointing to a hillock half a league away.

Caoimhe took a deep breath and squared her shoulders. "I am ready."

He kissed her forehead. "That's my brave girl," he said softly.

She smiled up at him. He was cataloguing her virtues so readily...what would he do when he discovered her faults? She only hoped they were things he could live with for eternity.

Holding hands, they slowly traveled the last distance to the rise. On the other side of the hill, facing west into the sunrise, was a natural shelter amongst the woven roots. It provided a break against the rising wind, and a carpet of fragrant leaves made a fair bed.

Ailill settled her into the hollow, her back against the root wall to take advantage of as much shelter as possible and then lay down beside her to keep her warm. "It is no' much, love, but it is the best I have to offer."

"'Tis better than the castle dungeon by half. I am content." She nestled into the crook of his arm, her head upon his breast.

They amused themselves by telling each other stories to explain the starry spangles in the sky. The constellations were not those she knew, but she made up offerings just the same, growing more and more outrageous in her fictions.

"And that one," she confided, pointing to a cluster of dim lights with two bright points in their midst, "is The Lovers. They are surrounded by obstacles but shine through the darkness for each other."

"They do, do they?" He chuckled deep in his chest.

She could feel the rumbling beneath her cheek and slapped at him playfully. "Yes, they do. If you watch them very closely, you can see them speaking to each other—see!" She pointed upward at the stars. "They alternate twinkling as they carry on their conversation."

Ailill laughed aloud. "You are a delightful dreamer, Caoimhe." His arm tightened around her in a quick hug.

"Am I dreaming, Ailill?" she asked softly. "Will I awake at home in bed with cobwebby recollections of Faerie glamour?"

He bent his head and kissed her lips. "Did *that* feel like glamour, beloved?"

"If it were, would I know it?" she replied, a teasing smile tugging her lips in the twilight.

"Good point." His face set in a mock gravity. "Well...I could pinch you," he offered.

"No, thank you! I believe you." She sighed, resting her hand on his. "It is no' the life I expected for myself—bedding beneath a tree with a Fae swain in the land of the Sidhe—but I would no' trade my lot for all the gold in the mortal kingdom."

"Already distancing yourself from the world of men, my love?"

"You have told me I can never return. I chose freely. My life will be with you, Ailill, be it mortal or immortal, it matters no'."

"I will do my best to live up to your trust, Caoimhe Sinclair." His arms came around her to hold her close.

She felt a feather-soft touch as his wing curled up to cover her like a cloak against the night chill. Let the morrow bring what it might. Tonight there would be peace.

Chapter Fifteen

The flying hooves and smooth gait of the aughisky lulled Aisling into a sort of waking dreamland. She didn't register the passing moor but seemed to be flying through the Sidhe barrow on a bright spring day, laughing with Ailill as they played a game of tag through the crystalline morning. The sunlight glittered on his white-gold head, and his wings sparkled. She remembered well the occasion. They had been so happy—two halves of the whole. Would she ever see him again? They had parted in anger.

It was her chief regret. If only she could apologize to him. Ask him to accept her choice and give her his blessing. Take word to her mother of her happiness... but it was unlikely. He would have returned to the barrow, and she would never again be welcome there. The tears began to flow again, slipping from her cheeks and flying into the night to scatter Faerie jewels amidst the moor grasses.

Black Tom chortled behind her back. "Tears, Fae? Practicing to be human, are ye? 'Twill take more than that to convince the Lady to grant yer boon. 'Tis no' so easily won, to become mortal. And only a fool would wish to lose eternity for the sake of a few years in the arms of a human. They are weak and stupid. Why would ye waste yerself so?"

"I have no call to discuss my plans with you, piskie. You are to get me to the Lady, no' be my confidante. I do no' have to speak to you. And I shan't."

The aughisky continued through the darkness, miles melting away beneath its feet. Now, her heart called images of Fergal to mind—his dark hair glistening in the noonday sun as he bent his head to listen to her, his delighted laugh as he enjoyed her wonder over his handiwork. One hand strayed to the belt around her waist. She would convince him *and* the Lady Rhiannon of her sincerity. She would become his wife, grow old and die in his arms. It was all she wanted from life.

"Dreaming again, ain't ye, Fae?" Black Tom crooned in her ear, his breath hot against her cheek and stinking of dead things. "By the time we reach the Court, yer mortal swain will like be ripped in two by the Lady's hounds. I hope they save me some bones to gnaw."

She reached back over her shoulder to slap at him. "Shut your mouth, you slimy runt. I will singe your eyebrows from your pockmarked face if I have to. I am ready to feed *you* to the Hunt, and don't think I willna."

The piskie sniffed. "Big talk, Fae."

She let the fire begin to limn her fingers.

He squealed, "All right! I believe ye. I will be silent." He subsided with a growl.

They continued on in silence. Aisling's eyes strained in the darkness, desperate to see the mound of the barrow. They had to be close—they had been traveling for an eternity.

The creature whinnied eagerly, stretching its neck forward as it galloped like the wind.

"It senses the Lady's stables," muttered Black Tom sulkily. "'Twill not be long now."

Sure enough, a dark shape loomed before them, a hulking ridge of jagged rock with a rough-hewn opening lit by ghastly green torches. On either side of the opening stood cadaverous wraiths in ancient bronze armor, wickedly gleaming pikes in their hands.

The aughisky neighed loudly, and one of the wraiths glided forward to catch its head. The helmet tipped upward, and eyeless sockets studied the passengers.

"You are expected," boomed the guard in a hollow voice that made Aisling's blood run cold.

She slid from the back of the aughisky, taking care not to touch the wraith. Ignoring Black Tom, she strode forward, feigning a confidence she didn't feel.

The other wraith nodded his head as she passed, gesturing with his free hand and parting the darkness of the barrow entrance.

Within the rock passage beyond glowed hundreds of the green torches, illuminating the scene in a sickly ghost light. The passage wound down into the hillside for several switchbacks before opening into a massive rock-hewn chamber.

Unlike Faerie, here there were no blue skies and growing things. Here there were massive stalagmites reaching to kiss their stalactite counterparts in flowstone pillars. Crystal outcroppings glittered wickedly in the torchlight, and pools of black water lay like jet mirrors throughout the cavern. The chamber was irregular, with many nooks and niches filled with monstrous creatures and darkly handsome Fae with pale skin and long black hair.

All eyes turned to Aisling as she walked into the chamber, and she heard the susurration of whispers swiftly running before her. Bold black stares greeted her, and bubbles skidded across some of the pools.

She continued forward, eyes fixed on the onyx throne across the expanse of the cavern. The chair seemed carved of a single stone, lifting to the ceiling in frozen waves and twisted forms. Its cushions were of blood-red velvet, and its fittings were gold. It was curiously beautiful.

Aisling barely saw the throne. Her eyes were fixed on the figure sitting upon it. Silver-blonde hair spilled in braids to Rhiannon's waist, and her skin was the cool cream of ivory. Only her golden girdle and the blood-red pendant resting upon her breast relieved the ebony velvet of her gown. At the foot of the throne rested two mastiffs the size of small ponies, and her long, pale fingers toyed with the beasts.

Halfway across the chamber, Aisling could feel the pull of those bottomless black eyes. She gulped down her heart and forced herself to keep moving. Only by calling on every ounce of will she possessed did she go smoothly to one knee in a deep curtsey, keeping the tremble from her limbs.

"My Lady, Rhiannon," she murmured.

"Rise, child," the Lady commanded with a gesture. Her voice was deep for a woman but melodic and surprisingly warm.

Aisling obeyed, clasping her hands before her to keep the trembling under control.

"You come to us under most interesting circumstances," continued the Lady. "Not at all what I expect from a Sidhe Fae. Especially one so closely allied with the Royal House."

Aisling bowed her head in acknowledgement of the Lady's statement. "'Tis true, my Queen. But I come here no' as a member of my House, but as a supplicant."

The Lady nodded. "Aye. I know why you have come. It is a foolish quest, young Aisling. Eternity is long, and you are little more than a hatchling. How can you know you wish to renounce your future? And for a man who may not live past morning?"

Aisling's heart skipped at the words. "I know what I know, Lady Rhiannon. Fergal O'Connor is the one I wish to spend my life with."

"Then do it, girl. Keep him as a pet, and when he is old and no longer pleases, replace him with another. There is no great stigma in doing so. Many of the Court do as much. Even the great Avallach has dallied with mortal mistresses when the fancy takes him. But to give up your immortality, to grow old, wither, and eventually die...that is too great a sacrifice. Rethink this folly."

"I have thought about it, my Lady. It is what I wish to do."

"Very noble," scoffed Rhiannon, her restless fingers tugging at the ear of her dog until it whined under her hand. "And were I to give in to this folly and grant what you desire, how would you pay for your gift? 'Tis not lightly given, and the cost must equal the favor. What are you willing to sacrifice to me?"

Aisling licked dry lips. "I have nothing of value, Lady. I throw myself upon your mercy."

Rhiannon laughed, a lilting girlish sound, which seemed incongruous in the dismal setting. "Mercy? Oh, you poor poppet. I have none." She leaned forward on her great throne. "Do you want to see my mercy in action, little Fae? Shall I show you what price I exact?"

She sat back in her throne and snapped her fingers. A cloaked figure that was strangely familiar to Aisling stepped forward with a bow.

"Fetch me my pet."

"As you command, Lady." The man turned to obey, a sneer on his handsome features. His hidden tunic flashed green for an instant in the wan torchlight.

Aisling's eyes widened with shock. One of the Dagda's trusted guards *here*, among the Unseelie? She must be mistaken.

The cloaked man returned, shoving another before him.

A tall, stooped form with a tangled mane of indifferent brown curls fading to gray stumbled forward. He looked up at the Lady wearily, and Aisling gasped.

He was a near copy of Tadhg.

"Thank you, Ruarc," said the Lady. "I can see I have gained a welcome ally in you."

"Your servant," replied Ruarc with a bow.

Aisling shuddered. A traitor from the Sidhe. Her life was turning on its head! She did not know what to think or who to trust any more.

"Rioghan, tell the little Fae your story," Rhiannon murmured, with a catlike smirk.

Rioghan flushed. His hands moved expressively, but he did not speak.

"Come, now—speak to our guest," chided the queen.

He opened his mouth, and Aisling realized with shock that his tongue had been cut out.

Rhiannon laughed again. This time the sound was not so childlike. "My pet displeases you? Shall I have him put to death? I grow weary of him anyway. There is too much of his mother in him. This is what being mortal is like, hatchling. He is far younger than you are, and look at him. A hapless wreck." She planted her foot on Rioghan's backside and pushed him until he stumbled forward out of reach.

"I had to slice out his tongue a fortnight after I brought him hither. He would not stop his incessant crying."

Aisling's heart went out to the poor baby stolen from his mother's side to grow up here in this loveless place. She stepped toward Rioghan, but he turned away.

"Ungrateful wretch!" spat Rhiannon. "How dare you insult my guest?" She gestured to one of the dogs, and it leapt upon the man, ripping his throat out.

"No!" Aisling screamed in horror, much to Rhiannon's amusement, but it was too late.

Rioghan's sightless eyes stared up at the rock above him from a pool of spreading blood as the dogs licked at the treat and began to worry the corpse. Aisling turned away, unable to watch.

"This is *my* Court, little Fae," murmured Rhiannon, leaning forward, her eyes glittering in the light of the ghostly torches. "What do you think of *my* world?"

Chapter Sixteen

Ailill woke to the sun in his face and a cramp in the wing he had used to blanket Caoimhe through the night. Slowly and carefully, he eased away from her, leaving her sleeping in the golden sunrise. He gazed down at her fondly. She was such a fragile little beauty. What had he done to deserve so wondrous a creature?

Rising to his feet, he stretched to his full height, wingtips quivering as they groped toward the sun. With one quick glance down at Caoimhe, he called on Fae magic and shrank to the size of a large butterfly.

Wings beating strong and sure, he flitted swiftly toward the nearest orchard grove he knew. Plucking pocketfuls of fruit for the remainder of their journey, he chided himself silently. Why hadn't he told her he could ease her hunger this easily last night? He was hiding many of his gifts from her...what was the reason?

He flew back to the hollow tree, arriving as Caoimhe's eyelids fluttered open. He greeted her with a smile and an extended *driw* fruit.

Her eyes widened, and she took the fruit. "Where did it come from?" she asked.

"There is an orchard nearby, we must have missed it in the dark," he answered evasively, hating himself for lying to her but still not quite ready to give up all his secrets.

She took a bite of the fruit and held it out to him.

He shook his head with a smile. "It's for you. I have more. We won't go hungry again."

She tucked a strand of hair behind one ear and bit into the *driw* again. "This is delicious," she sighed. "I could eat these forever."

"Good. Because it will be a staple of your diet."

Caoimhe laughed. "I suppose it will be." She shook her head. "There is so much to learn."

He reached down a hand as she finished the fruit and carefully placed the pit on a root where one of the planter birds could find it. "Come," he said gently, "it is time we moved on."

She paled but laid her hand in his and allowed herself to be pulled to her feet. Dusting away the leaves clinging to her skirts, she nodded. "I am ready."

He flexed his wings and slipped his arm around her waist. "It isn't too far now."

They walked on in silence. The groves of twisted trees grew thicker, branches weaving overhead into a ceiling of black lace with blue backing. Beams of sunlight stabbed down in pinpoint spots of warm gold, highlighting gilt and crimson leaves in piles like tossed cushions in a salon.

"The Morrigan's waiting room," Ailill whispered to Caoimhe. "Look sharp, and you may spot other supplicants."

She started and moved a little closer.

"I'm only teasing, love," he soothed. "We are still some distance from the castle. But I truly believe we have nothing to worry on, Caoimhe. She is distant kin and a gentle being when she wishes to be. There is no reason to fear her."

"It is so eerie, Ailill. I feel eyes watching us."

"'Tis the ravens. They are the eyes of the Morrigan.

Through them, she sees all and knows much. She will be expecting us."

"Will she know why we have come?"

"Quite likely. It wouldn't be too difficult to guess why we've come when the ravens have watched our every step, from the Dagda's castle to hers."

"I see." Caoimhe seemed to shrink into herself, shoulders slumping and head down.

"Don't worry, love. I am sure she will listen fairly."

"And why should she?" croaked a rusty voice.

Startled, Ailill stepped in front of Caoimhe, spreading his wings protectively.

There was a cackling laugh from above them, and both craned their necks upward. "Look at the little Fae strut."

Sitting in the wizened branches of the ancient hollow oak before them was a huge raven, dusty black wings highlighted with green and blue as a beam of sunlight struck its feathers. It cocked its head, one glittering golden eye fixing them with a quizzical stare. "And what have we here? A mortal! In Faerie? What trick is this?"

It flapped its wings and then sailed down to the leaf-strewn ground before them. Its head swiveled from side to side, studying each in turn. "Oh, bother!" grated the bird. "It is too difficult to see you like this."

There was a crack of thunder and a flash of light. When the rumble died, the raven was gone. In its place stood a tall Fae woman in a scarlet dress with an iridescent black cloak wrapped close around her. Waves of russet hair flowed to her waist, and her golden eyes twinkled in the depths of her hood, under a headdress of black feathers with a golden beak. Her wings, unlike Ailill's transparent, wispy, ethereal things, were solid and feathered like a raven's. They curled outside her cloak, lifting and falling slightly as she stood beaming at them.

"My Lady," cried Ailill, sinking down on one knee, head bowed.

"Oh, do get up Ailill Brightwing. Your mortal love knows not what to think and trembles like an aspen."

She stepped forward, holding out a graceful white hand to Caoimhe. "Manners were ever the boy's shortcoming. I am Anu, whom they call the Morrigan. Who might you be, my lovely child?"

Before he could warn her, Caoimhe dropped a pretty curtsey and replied, "My name is Caoimhe Sinclair, Lady."

A triumphant smirk quirked the Morrigan's lip, but she answered gravely, "It is a pleasure to meet you, my dear. You are far from home. What brings you hither?"

Ailill interrupted before Caoimhe could answer. "We seek your guidance, Lady. And crave a boon."

"I see. Well, standing out here in the sunlight is bad for the complexion. I wish to talk more to our guest, but this is not the place. Do come inside." She waved her hand, and the ancient oak split down the middle with a deafening crack.

Caoimhe gasped in surprise.

Anu laughed. She placed her hands together, palm to palm before her, and whispered a charm. Spreading her hands wide, she cried aloud, "*Adira!*" and the tree creaked open like a double-winged doorway. The top steps of a set of broad stone stairs could be seen in the shadows. "Come," the Morrigan invited. "It is much more comfortable inside my keep."

She lifted her hand above her head and called forth a purple-tinged ball of Fae fire. Holding it aloft like a torch, she led the way down the steps.

Ailill took a firm grip on Caoimhe's hand and stepped forward, setting booted foot on the top riser. "All will be well, love," he whispered, and wished he had greater faith it was true.

Caoimhe nodded with a quick little smile and followed him out of the sunlight.

The stairway wound down for what seemed an eternity, spiraling deeper and deeper into the earth. Finally, they reached the bottom, the stairs ending before a wide, earthen tunnel.

The Fae fire gave off plenty of light to see their way, but not enough to illuminate all the shadows. Caoimhe clung to his side.

Ailill drew himself up. She was counting on him to be brave for them both. Very well, he would be. He curled his wing around her for comfort.

They traveled almost half a league in the dim tunnel before a second set of stairs loomed in front of them. Instead of the rough hewn stone that had led them hither, these steps were smooth white marble seeming to glow in the purple light. A delicate banister wrought of golden fretwork curved down each side of the stairway.

At the top of the steps was an arched doorway of etched gold, its pattern two trees with intertwined branches. In the center of the net formed of the woven branches sat a raven, its wings outstretched.

As Anu approached the golden door, it split down the center, halving the raven. It swung backward silently, and she paused in the opening.

"Well come to my castle," she intoned. "May all enter freely and go in peace."

She gestured to the interior, and Ailill mounted the last of the stairs to stand upon the landing. He bowed his head slightly and escorted Caoimhe through the doorway.

He heard her sharp intake of breath as she caught her first glimpse of the Morrigan's throne room and smiled. He had reacted much the same on his first sight of it. He glanced around him, seeing it again as if for the first time.

The room was huge and precisely square. Walls of polished marble rose like white canvas sails to a height of ten spans then arched to meet in a domed ceiling. A heavy chandelier hung from the center of the dome on a twisted golden chain, dozens of tapers casting their glow on the room below. Tiny sprites hovered around the candles on rainbow wings, making sure the lights stayed lit and the wicks trimmed.

All about the perimeter of the walls were gilt lounges piled with thick velvet cushions in brilliant hues. Greens, purples, crimsons, and gold glowed against the white walls and gilded furniture.

Dominating the room was a three-step dais with a great golden chair upon it. The back of the chair was crafted in the shape of the same raven that graced the doorway. Its huge wings were unfurled in a ten-foot span.

Anu climbed the steps to her throne and settled upon it. With a flick of her wrist, she dispelled the ball of Fae fire.

"Now, let's speak of why you have come," she began

with no preamble. "I have something you hope to convince me to return."

She snapped her fingers, and a group of the tiny sprites brought forth a velvet stool to rest beneath her feet. She clapped her hands, and another Fae came forward—this one a tall, fair-haired youth with wings furled tightly against his shoulder blades. In his hand, he carried a scarred oak harp.

He sat on the step at the Lady's feet, and his slender fingers began to dance across the strings of his instrument, calling forth mental images of cool streams and dazzling sunlight.

"May I present to you Uaithne?" the Morrigan continued. "Why in the name of Faerie would I want to give him back?"

CHAPTER SEVENTEEN

I've made a horrible mistake, Aisling thought. Her stomach roiled in reaction to the carnage she had just witnessed. Rhiannon was as cold and unfeeling as she was beautiful. She would never understand love or sacrifice. *And I've delivered Fergal into her hands.* The thought knifed through her, bringing a gasp to her lips.

"What is the matter, pretty one?" Rhiannon clucked, her mad eyes blazing in pretended sympathy. "Are you ill? Does the sight of blood offend your delicate sensibilities? Very well."

She called out in a harsh, throaty language filled with jaw-cracking syllables and guttural sounds. A scrabble of goblins descended on the dogs, kicking at the beasts with their horny feet and snarling back at the animals. One of them bit the bitch on her ear, and the dog retreated to her side of the throne with a whimper. Rhiannon comforted her with an absent pat.

The swarthy little men bundled what was left of Rioghan into a pile and then scooped the tortured remains up in their arms. They huddled together, conversing in their vile language, coming to some kind of decision.

One of them turned to Rhiannon and asked her a question in the same cruel-sounding tongue.

She laughed in delight and turned to Aisling. "How polite they are! They wish to know if you want them to save you something for dinner or if they can eat the whole corpse. Isn't that sweet?"

Aisling swallowed hard, refusing to be baited. "Extend my thanks, but I have eaten."

Rhiannon's eyes narrowed, and then her smile was back. "Very well. Your loss." She turned to the leader of the goblins and barked out a command.

The creature bowed low to the throne and then to Aisling. Swiping one last bit of the poor unfortunate Rioghan off the stone floor, he led his scrabble back into the shadows, where a bloodstained curtain closed off an alcove. They disappeared behind the drapery.

Aisling fought to ignore the grunts and belches filtering out from their feast. "Where is Fergal?" she asked in a breathless whisper, unable to bear the suspense any longer.

"Fer—oh, yes! Your little mortal..." Rhiannon pretended to contemplate the question. "Hmmm... where did I put him? Did I give him to the goblins? No, they have far too good an appetite to have dined already on human meat. Was it the bogies? No...no. I believe they are off on an errand this night. Perhaps— wait! I remember." She sat up, clapping her hands delightedly. "I told Jack to give him to the Hunt."

Aisling's blood ran cold, and she felt light-headed as panic drove her to her knees. "You what?"

Rhiannon's eyes were now two focused pools of hate. "I gave him to the Hunt. It's been too long since my Court has had a worthy quarry. And here we have an upstart mortal who seeks to enter my Kingdom—*my* Kingdom— and steal away a member of the Seelie royal house. Distant relation perhaps but nobility still. How could I let such a thing happen? I am a loyal Sidhe. I could not stand by and let such arrogance go unpunished."

"It was my idea," Aisling murmured. She felt a tear slide down her cheek to tinkle on the stone below despite her efforts to control her emotions. "Call them back. Let Fergal return home. I will do whatever you say."

"Isn't she precious?" Rhiannon asked her Court of monsters. Most of them were too dull-witted to understand what she was asking, but they all smiled and nodded, knowing the high cost of her displeasure. "Sycophants!" she snarled.

Aisling begged the Queen to reconsider. "Please, Lady. I will face the Hunt, but let Fergal return to the ones who love him."

"Come, come, child, you can't have it both ways. How can you entertain the Hunt *and* Fergal return to his loved ones? It is obvious *you* are one of those loved ones. Though to come here alone and bring me no gift, no treasure, no offering of any kind is hardly the way to prove it. If you truly wanted to convince me to take away your wings, you should have come better prepared.

"Did you ask Tadhg to describe the process to you? Did he tell you *how* I take your wings? Do you think it is some magical wave of the hand, and they disappear? Poof! And you are mortal?" She sneered in wicked pleasure at the thought.

"No, my girl. It is a ripping, tearing, amputation. I slice the wings from your living flesh with an iron dagger. The iron insures they will not re-grow as they would normally do. You really should have asked Tadhg to show you his back, where the scars of the removal still stand as furrows, nearly a century after their taking. And when the wings are gone, you are not mortal—merely maimed Fae—until the ritual is complete. Until I take your very essence from the blood in your veins. Until I burn away your powers one by one and leave you an empty husk writhing upon the floor. Is *that* what you want, little Fae?" She spat out the last words like venom.

Aisling kept her chin high. "If that is what it takes— yes. 'Tis what I want."

Rhiannon sat back in her chair, a look of surprise on her cold features. "You love him enough that you would face all of that to be mortal at his side? What a foolish little thing you are..."

"Mayhap you are right...but it is my choice to make."

"Aye. 'Tis your choice." Rhiannon leaned toward her again, licking her lips with the tip of her pink tongue. "But there is still the matter of my fee. It is customary for a mortal to bring me a trinket of great price merely to be allowed into my presence. I waive the fee for your precious swain...though one of you indeed shall be quarry for my Hunt before the week is out. However, I cannot forego the price of your mortality. If I grant you your heart's desire, what shall you give *me*?"

"I have told you before," Aisling answered wearily, her voice dull with despair. "I have nothing to offer you."

Rhiannon cocked her head, her cold profile waxen in the light of the ghost torches. "I could ask of you the same I asked of Tadhg...your firstborn child—it could become a sort of standard price for the service— but somehow, I doubt you would be willing to pay it, considering how his payment ended." She ruffled the fur of one of the dogs with her dainty foot.

It opened one red eye to half-mast and growled through bloodstained fangs.

Rhiannon giggled.

"No. I don't think such a demand would work. You are far too softhearted. With Tadhg, he didn't think twice. I suppose it is the mothering instinct that makes a female so protective. Goodness knows my own Pryderi caused me nothing but trouble. I was happy to be rid of him. Perhaps it is the very mortality you seek that makes an infant seem so precious. Even amongst the Fae not all hatchlings survive. Hmmm...a subject to ponder." She tapped her chin with one long finger as if in contemplation.

"But not today. Today, I must think of an appropriate gift for you to offer."

Her eyes lit up, and her mouth formed an "O" of delighted surprise. "I have it! Oh, yes. That will do. Along with your wings, you shall give me your beauty. Then the truth will out. If Fergal is worthy of the sacrifice you make, it will not matter to him if you are fair or no. He will love you, even if you are hideous.

"If he is false—as most males and all mortal men come to prove in time—you will have learned a valuable lesson to comfort you in your mortality."

She preened, pleased with her decision. "Come, hither, little Fae," she cooed, crooking a finger at Aisling.

Aisling crept forward, taking care not to step in the congealing blood staining the stone before the throne. As she drew closer to the chair, and actually looked at it, she could interpret more detail. It was shaped like an immense shadow dragon, head lifted and onyx flames shooting from its open mouth. Rubies glittered in the eye sockets—each the size of robin's eggs. The gold fittings were slave manacles about its hocks, and what she had taken for waves were the sweeps of its mighty wings, half-furled, as if it were ready to leap aloft.

It was easier to focus on the throne than its occupant. She dreaded what Rhiannon was about to do. Only the thought of Fergal kept her from throwing herself to the ground and begging to be forgiven—to be ignored for a foolish hatchling. But the image of the mortal rose in her mind, and she stood before the queen, shoulders back—awaiting what was to come.

"First the wings, I think," said Rhiannon, with a thoughtful pout, pulling a black dagger from her sleeve and taking care not to contact the blade directly. "Turn your back to me."

Aisling did as she was bid, steeling herself.

She felt a cool hand take hold of one wing just above the point where it joined her back. She gasped.

"Here goes nothing," purred Rhiannon's voice.

A searing pain lanced down Aisling's back as she felt the iron blade slice through muscle and bone. The iron burned like fire, adding its damage to the cut itself. She screamed.

"And another."

The second wing was cut from her back, and she pitched forward onto her face, mindless from the pain. Her fingers clutched at the stone beneath her, slippery with Rioghan's blood and now her own.

"We're not finished, little girl," Rhiannon warned, nudging her onto her back with the toe of one black velvet shoe. "This is only the beginning."

The black dagger slashed forward in two quick cuts before Aisling could think and lay open both cheeks to the bone.

CHAPTER EIGHTEEN

"I thought the Dagda said he bet his *harp* in the wager," Ailill blurted out.

"He did," replied Anu. "The harper was an extra added bonus."

"But, he said the *harp* was Uaithne—"

"It is. And so is the harper. And the interior rhyme scheme of poetry itself. A paucity of names, it seems." Her voice dripped amusement. Her fingers twined in the bard's golden hair, and he smiled up at her fondly. "Uaithne and I have become quite...close. I see no reason to give up his friendship because Avallach has had a change of heart."

"But, Lady—the harp itself is the key to the flow of life. 'Tis the waning days of summer. If the Dagda does no' play in the change of seasons, the mortal realm will begin to die."

"What concern is that of mine?"

"Please, my Lady," Caoimhe began tentatively, "I can see your reasons for denying the Dagda's request. He did a foolish thing in wagering so precious an object. But should my entire world fade into the twilight because of one being's folly? I beg you to reconsider."

The Morrigan looked not unkindly on Caoimhe but shook her head with a sad smile. "I am sorry for your loss, my dear, but your moving words are not enough to persuade me. If for no other reason than to persuade the old fool to be more careful in future, I cannot give in on this. Your world means little to me, and its loss will affect me not."

"What about the loss of your own world?" asked Ailill.

"What do you mean, boy?"

"Caoimhe is a mortal. Already Faerie is beginning to resent her presence. Only by eating of a golden apple can she remain here as an accepted resident. But she has eaten of the *driw*, as well as the Dagda's stew, and cannot return to the mortal realm, as well you know. Faerie will die if she lives and does no' get her immortality—which the Dagda will only grant in exchange for the harp."

The Morrigan's eyes narrowed, and suddenly, she didn't seem so gracious. "It seems to me there is a simple way to solve all the problems at once," she murmured, a dangerous edge to her voice. "Merely remove the source of the difficulty."

Ailill stepped in front of Caoimhe protectively. "You would have to come through me, and we both know what would happen to our world if one Seelie Fae killed another."

She sat back on her throne with an audible growl of displeasure. "It would destroy Faerie in a heartbeat. It seems we are at an impasse." She glowered at Caoimhe. "All for the sake of a pretty face and a boyish libido."

Ailill felt his face grow hot. "You know nothing of love."

"And you do?" The Morrigan rolled her eyes in disbelief. "You've known this child, what—two days, three? And you are willing to sacrifice our *entire* Kingdom—ancient before her ancestors set foot upon this isle—because you 'love' her? Your wings must be the only bright things about you!"

Uaithne—who had played on throughout the

conversation, seemingly oblivious to the world around him—cleared his throat. "I have a suggestion, my Lady."

"What is it?" she snapped.

He looked up at her reprovingly, emerald eyes hooded behind golden lashes.

She paled under his stare, lowering her eyes. She replied meekly, "I am sorry. Please, what would you suggest?"

Ailill was surprised by the exchange. Perhaps Anu knew something of love after all...

Uaithne set aside the oaken harp and rose to his feet. He took the Morrigan's hand in his and raised it to his lips, kissing it fondly. "Thank you for the opportunity to speak, my Lady."

A pretty blush bloomed on her cheeks, and she nodded graciously. "Do tell us your suggestion, my Lord."

Uaithne turned to Ailill. "You say the Dagda mentioned only the return of the harp in his behest?"

"Aye."

"And you, my Lady," Uaithne said to Anu, a smile lighting his narrow features, "you do no' really care for a thing of wood, do you? I flatter myself 'tis the *harper* you desire."

"True..." she answered slowly.

"My proposal is this, my Queen. Let these children take Uaithne the Harp back to the Dagda with your compliments—it will show your magnanimous nature and strength of character. In return, Uaithne the Harper will remain at your Court—and your side—as long as you have need of him."

Ailill heard Caoimhe's indrawn breath behind him. It was a beautiful solution to the problem...would the

Morrigan accept it?

"An interesting proposal," the Lady said thoughtfully. "I will consider it. It is time for luncheon. After we have eaten, I will give my answer."

She stood, offering her hand to Uaithne once more. "Come, we will speak of this further in my chamber over the meal." As they exited the room, she called back over her shoulder. "There is a banquet laid in the dining hall. Sit and eat, the sprites will attend you." And then they were gone.

"Do you think she will give us the harp, Ailill?" asked Caoimhe, her voice hushed and breathless as she clutched at his sleeve.

"She already has," he replied with a grin. "It would lose her face to come right out and say so, but she has left the room, the harp, and us alone together. I do no' expect she intends to find more than one of the three present when she returns."

Caoimhe giggled nervously. "Do you really think she wishes us to steal it away?"

"It is fitting to her nature." He stepped to the dais, running a hand over the worn oak of the harp.

The harp was a beautiful thing. The honey-colored wood almost glowed. It felt silken smooth under his touch, polished by centuries of use. Its pillar was carved to resemble a double-headed fish with glittering sapphires for eyes, and the strings were fine gold wire.

As he stroked the silky wood, one of the fish heads swiveled to peer up at him. "Do you wish to hear a song, my Lord?" it asked, in a voice like liquid bubbling up through stone.

Ailill jumped back.

"It talks!" Caoimhe gasped.

The fish head swung to glance her way. "Yes, *he* talks. And he is quite intelligent enough to have his own opinion on these proceedings, thank you very much."

"I beg your pardon, good harp," she apologized, dropping a pretty little curtsey. "Where I come from, only humans talk."

"Yes, and badly for the most part," sniffed the fish. "The stories I could tell you...but I digress." A ripple seemed to run through its shining scales. "It is time we were going home."

Ailill stepped closer once more. "Are you agreeing we should be off before the Morrigan returns?"

"Unless you wish to wait until my counterpart has successfully satisfied the wench, and from what I've seen, it can take the rest of the day." The fish sounded impatient. "Come now, grab a handful of viands for the journey, and let's get on our way. You, mortal, there is a basket on the lounge behind the throne. The Morrigan told you—the table in the next room is laid for luncheon—go see what you can find. And be sure to bring some breadcrumbs for me. It is a long way back to the crystal keep."

Obediently, Caoimhe retrieved the basket and tiptoed into the next room to do the harp's bidding.

As soon as she had left the chamber, the fish returned its stare to Ailill. "Fool! What were you thinking? Or are you? To bring a mortal into Faerie is not something to be done lightly. It is not something to be done in haste. Frankly, it is not something to be done *at all*! Look at the trouble you have caused already, and you've scarce known her two days—"

"But I—"

"—And don't flap your gills at me about love! You haven't known her long enough to know her favorite color, much less love her."

"I do love her," Ailill protested, hands balling to fists at his sides.

"Oh, please," scoffed the fish. "How old are you, boy, that you are still so naïve?"

"I am one hundred and twenty, thing of wood. Old enough and plenty to know my own mind."

"I am not so sure you have a mind. Seems to me you are thinking with your hot blood and not your cool head."

"I don't know why no one believes I can possibly love Caoimhe, but it is true. *I* believe it, and that is all that matters!"

The fish stared at him for a moment and then broke into bubbling chuckles. "'Tis well then. But it had to be said. Had to be sure. This is a nice place. I don't have to sing for battles any more, no drunken brawls or petty gambling. I could happily remain with the harper. But I will come with you—for the sake of love."

Ailill bowed to the harp.

Caoimhe returned from the dining hall, her basket heaped with bread and cheese and the dark purple *driw*. She smiled at him.

Ailill felt as if his heart would burst. This beautiful creature had given up everything for him. It was a gift he must prove himself worthy of.

"Let's be off," warned the harp. "The Morrigan is a flighty creature at times and could change her mind at any moment. If she catches us here, she will keep me for spite."

Lifting the instrument carefully, Ailill nodded. "We will return you to the Dagda at once, and all will be set right."

Uaithne chortled. "You can dream, hatchling, but things will never be set back to the way they were. You are changing Faerie forever. For good or ill, I cannot say, but it will never be the same."

CHAPTER NINETEEN

Aisling came to her senses in a world of fire and pain. She lay facedown on a slab of stone beneath guttering torches casting flickering red and gold tongues of flame to reflect in the polished rock. Her back was an agony of licking fire, and she wondered dully if a torch had caught her wings, until memory caught up with her. She had no wings. It was done.

Slowly and carefully, she eased into a sitting position, gasping as the tortured flesh broke open and began to bleed again. She started to drop her face into her hands and then remembered the rest. Tentatively, she touched first one cheek and then the other. The disfiguring wounds ran from the corners of her eyes to nearly touch her nose. The scars would be prominent.

The thought brought tears to her eyes, and she began to cry. But instead of the Faerie tears that usually fell to the ground in tinkling cascades of semi-precious stone, these tears were large drops of water that burned the crusted cuts on her cheeks with new fire.

"What has happened to me?" she wailed.

"Seems to me you've received your heart's desire. You've gotten what you wished for, foolish spirit," came a soft, sibilant voice from the shadows.

Aisling cringed back against the wall, heedless of the fresh pain from her back. "Who is there?"

"Do no' worry so, small one. I am no' your enemy. Though no' your friend, either. I merely am me."

"Show yourself!"

"Are you so sure you sincerely wish to see me?"

"I do no' fear you."

"Perhaps you should..."

The conversation was taking her mind off the pain, and Aisling leaned towards the voice. "Come out. Please."

There was a soft sigh, and a shadowy shape detached itself from the looming rocks, stealing forward cautiously. Standing about five feet in height, the figure was female, small breasted and sharp-featured. She was nude, though her tangled mane of mouse-brown hair nearly reached her waist. She hunkered down on the floor in front of Aisling's perch, hugging her knees.

"Who are you?" asked Aisling. "Are you a prisoner here like me?"

"You are no prisoner, silly one. You may stay or go as you please."

"I may?"

"Yes, of course. The Lady merely placed you here to rest—you were once Fae, after all. Your wounds are grave. There was a chance of fever. Still is, if you are foolish enough to slip away."

"You still haven't told me your name," Aisling prodded.

"No' so quick to give my name as some," sniffed the creature. "I know my boundaries, and I stay within them, I do. 'Twould have been wise of others no' to be so free with their true names. Too much power given with a name. I am a gwyllion. 'Tis enough to know."

Aisling nodded. She knew stories of these solitary mountain Faeries, with their odd habit of sitting motionless in the rocks to either side of a path to silently spy on passing travelers. But she had never heard of them being malicious.

"Am I mortal now?" she whispered to the gwyllion.

Gwyllion shrugged. "Mortal or nearly so. The Lady keeps her word. She took your wings and took your beauty, so she gave you what you bargained for. I do no' know if she is through with you, but 'tis no' my place to know."

Aisling felt a sense of wonder. She was no longer Fae. The Lady had given her what she asked. She could stay with Fergal—Fergal...where was he?

"Do you know where Fergal is, Gwyllion?"

"Who?"

"The man the Lady had brought here. The mortal."

Gwyllion cocked her head. "Why bother?"

"What do you mean?" Aisling's blood ran cold.

"He is to run before the Wild Hunt. The black hounds always get their quarry. He will be dead by dawn."

Aisling slid off the ledge of rock, catching herself on the edge as her knees buckled beneath her. "I must go to him."

"Why?" Gwyllion asked curiously.

Aisling stared at the little creature. The gwyllion honestly didn't see any reason why Aisling would want to find Fergal. It was sad, really.

"I love him," she answered simply.

"What is 'love'?"

"It makes the heart sing...it is the greatest gift two beings can share...it is what makes life worth living."

"Sounds very foolish to me," shrugged Gwyllion. "But if you must see the mortal one, I can take you to him."

"Please," begged Aisling eagerly.

The gwyllion rose to its feet. "Come with me."

Every step was an agony. The tattered shreds of her filmy dress stuck to the bloody wounds where her wings had been. When she walked, the movement of her muscles caused the fragile fabric to shift and pull. Her mutilated cheeks throbbed with a bone-deep ache. What would Fergal say when he saw the ruin of her face?

The hallway through which they walked was dank and dark, little more than a low tunnel through the rock. The neglected torches sputtered at intervals of thirty or forty feet, barely illuminating the rough floor.

Aisling began to grope her way along the walls, trying to avoid catching her bare feet on the rough stone walkway. "Slow down," she pleaded. "I cannot move so quickly."

Gwyllion rolled her eyes and sighed heavily. "Such a fool. All your own fault. What a shame."

"Perhaps," Aisling murmured, taking advantage of the pause to rest her feet and ease her shoulders. "It was my decision to make."

"Worth it?"

"To me it was. To me it was worth everything."

The gwyllion shook its head. "Foolish. Nearly there."

Aisling pushed away from the wall. She could sense time running out. "Let's be on our way."

They walked on for another half league, and then Gwyllion stopped before an ironbound door. "He lies behind this door, foolish Fae-no-more. Be quick with your goodbyes. The Wild Hunt will ride within the hour." She faded away like smoke.

Aisling tugged frantically at the door, but it would not open.

"Fergal!" she whispered apprehensively, nervously glancing around for watching eyes. "Fergal, are you there?"

There was the sound of movement from beyond the door, and then she heard his voice. "Aisling? Is it you? Whatever possessed you to come here, girl? Go back to Faerie before it is too late."

"I can't go back there. It's too late already."

"What do you mean?"

"It's done. I've already seen the White Lady. My wings are gone. I'm mortal now."

"Aisling!" His voice was filled with a curious mixture of sorrow and shock. "What have you done?"

"I've done what we set out to do, Fergal. I gave up my immortality."

"I told you it was too great a price!"

"And it was mine to pay." Her heart sank within her. He would never accept or understand. It had all been in vain.

She straightened her shoulders as best she could. All right then. She would see him home safely and then make her own way for the remainder of her days. Perhaps Tadhg could help her find someplace to set up housekeeping...or...

"Aisling?"

"Yes?" she mumbled, feeling the tears beginning to rise again and hastily willing them not to fall. The salt on her cuts would be the final straw. She could not bear it.

"Can you open the door?"

"I tried, but I can't pull it."

"Is it locked?"

"What is locked?"

Fergal sighed gustily. "Sorry, dear one. I forgot. Does it have a bar across the opening, or something through the handle?"

She scanned the doorway. There did seem to be a thick wooden beam resting between two iron fittings. The beam crossed the line of the doorway.

"There is a piece of wood lying across it."

"Can you lift it?"

"I can try."

"That's my clever girl. Lift it and slip it to the side so the door is free to open."

She struggled with the heavy beam but finally managed to knock it free of the iron hooks. It clattered to the stone floor, the sound echoing in the stillness.

"Quiet!" Fergal hissed.

She froze, hands to mouth. *What have I done?* She darted a frantic glance around the hallway, but it remained empty and silent.

"Did anyone hear?" he asked anxiously.

"I-I don't think so."

"Good. Now, can you open the door?"

She yanked on the handle. Without the bar, the door flew open on well-oiled hinges. Aisling lost her balance and fell backwards onto the hard stone floor. She cried out involuntarily as her mangled back slammed into the rock. She lay stunned from the pain.

Fergal stumbled out of the cell to kneel beside her, one hand covering her mouth. His clothes were nearly as tattered as her own, and there was a mad glitter in his dark eyes, eerily reminiscent of the White Lady.

"Quiet, fool!" he ordered. His gaze slid from one end of the hallway to the other.

She moaned beneath his hand as he continued to press down upon her wounded cheekbones.

With an incoherent oath, he let go of her. Rising to his feet, he pulled her to hers.

"Sorry."

"It's all right," she whispered, biting her lip against the throbbing ache.

Fergal bent down to peer intently at her face. "By all things holy, Aisling, what has happened to you?"

"I believe I can answer your question," drawled the voice of Rhiannon from over his shoulder. "I was just coming to fetch you. It is time for the Hunt. You may play as well, little one. The hounds are hungry enough for two."

Chapter Twenty

Ailill pushed them hard on the way back to the crystal keep, driven by some indefinable urgency. One eye measured the path of the sun to the horizon, and he moved faster yet as the gap narrowed.

Caoimhe kept her silence, sensing there was something bothering him. She did her best to keep up with his pace while fighting through a stitch in her side. She tried to keep her gasps of pain to herself.

The harp was not as thoughtful. "What is the hurry, hatchling?" huffed Uaithne. "The crystal does not melt in the rain. The keep will still be standing when we arrive in good time."

Ailill did not answer him but hurried onward so quickly his wings were almost lifting him off the ground.

Caoimhe stumbled as her bare foot caught on a protruding root. She bit back a cry of pain as she lost her balance, going to one knee in the path.

The sound of her cry stopped Ailill at last. He turned and lifted her gently to her feet.

"Are you all right, beloved?" he asked with an anxious tinge to his voice. He sat her down on a nearby stump and set the harp on the ground beside it. "We'll rest here a moment," he conceded, kneeling down and taking her foot into his hand. Examining the bruised toe and bloodied knee, he clucked his tongue and concentrated his healing on the injuries. A warm glow limned his hands with a dim golden light as he concentrated. "This should help ease the pain."

"Yes, thank you," she smiled down at him. Her hand reached as if to smooth the wayward hair from his forehead but stopped. It didn't seem appropriate for Faerie. Her heart lurched. Things would be different. She would lose many of the things she took for granted along with her mortality...but she would gain so much more.

Ailill sighed, sinking to the ground in a tailor-sit. He wrapped his arms around his knees. "Something is wrong, Caoimhe. I don't know what it is. I feel it, but I can't tell where the trouble is. My heart is heavy."

"We can go on."

Ailill shook his head. "No. It is getting late. It will be too dark to see the path soon." He got restlessly to his feet, pacing before her. "I can't describe it. There is a tremor in the ether. I haven't felt like this since—" He went dead still. "No!" he whispered.

Caoimhe sprang to her feet, coming over to lay a hand on his arm. "What is it, Ailill? You are pale as a ghost."

"The only time I've ever felt anything remotely like this is when my sister Aisling was injured in an accident. She broke her wing and could no' get home. I felt her pain. I was the only one who believed there was something wrong. I found her and carried her back to the aerie..."

"Do you feel the same now? Something is wrong with Aisling?"

"I'm no' sure. It is different. There is such a sense of urgency. I don't know..." He smiled down at her, but it was a half-hearted effort. "We are twins, you know. Some things cannot be explained."

"We *should* go on then."

"No, sweeting." He shook his head. "Let's find some shelter for the night. It should be a much more pleasant rest tonight, with the food from the Morrigan."

"Perhaps I can ease your mind," murmured Uaithne softly. "There is nothing you can do tonight, as you say, hatchling. There is a hollow beneath that hill." The harp's heads swiveled to the left. "It will be sheltered from the wind. Rest and eat. After you have supped, I will entertain you."

"I don't know if—" Ailill began.

"—No argument, hatchling. 'Tis an order."

Caoimhe hid a smile. "Come, beloved. 'Tis good advice." She took his hand and led him to the indicated hillock.

There was indeed a small hollow beneath the hill. They sat in companionable silence as they ate the bread and cheese Caoimhe had brought, finishing with the juicy *driw* fruit.

After the simple meal, Ailill curled his wing around her protectively.

She rested her head on his shoulder with a sigh.

Uaithne began to play softly, his strings moving of their own accord. At first, the music was formless; the sound of babbling water over sun-warmed rock. Then the music shifted. It became joyful and triumphant, lifting their hearts as the *geantrai*—the strain of merriment—echoed through the twilight. Subtly, the music shifted once more into the *suantrai*, or sleep-strain, and Ailill felt his eyelids growing heavy.

Caoimhe slept, her head heavy upon his shoulder.

He eased her to a more comfortable position, her head resting on his thigh. He tried to keep his eyes open, but the magic of the music won out, and he fell into a deep slumber.

* * *

Sometime in the night, he was jolted awake by a knifing pain, which made him cry out in agony. His back was on fire.

Caoimhe sat up with a start. "What is it, Ailill?"

He couldn't answer. Waves of pain washed through him, doubling him over, fingers scrabbling in the dirt. His brain felt as if it were under assault from some outside presence. As the pain crested and began to fall, new agony slashed across his cheeks.

Caoimhe put her arms around his trembling shoulders, holding him as closely as she dared. "Beloved, what is wrong?"

"Pain..." he gasped. "Such pain!" Tears slipped down his cheeks like jewels and pattered to the dirt as dusty jewels. "My wings..." He moaned deep in his throat, like a wounded animal.

"Your wings are fine," she soothed.

"They are on fire!"

"Love, there is nothing wrong."

Uaithne strummed a jangling chord. "Do not be so sure, little mortal. There is a great disturbance here—physically there may be no damage to the hatchling, but there is definitely something wrong."

"What do you mean, Lord Uaithne?" asked the girl softly. The harp commanded her respect by sheer virtue of his magic. Scarce days ago, she would have scoffed at tales of talking harps and winged lovers as dreams and fantasies. Now, her life would be among the Fae—for eternity.

"He is a twin. In your world, are there such?"

"Aye," she answered with a trace of amusement. "I have heard of such siblings."

"Do they also have a sympathetic bond? In Faerie, when such a rare birth occurs, the twins are so in-tune they can complete each other's thoughts. Aisling must be in trouble."

"I must go to her," Ailill gasped. "She needs me."

"Do you even know where she may be, young one? Patience. First to the Dagda. He may know more."

"You're right. We cannot wait any longer. We must go on." Ailill rose slowly to his feet, leaning on Caoimhe's shoulder.

Taking a deep breath, he centered himself. With a sideways glance at Caoimhe, he called a ball of Faerie fire into his hand.

Caoimhe gasped in wonder.

"Carry the harp, love. I must concentrate to keep the fire alight."

Obediently, Caoimhe tucked the harp under one arm and her basket over the other. She clambered to her feet awkwardly.

Ailill strode forward into the night, not glancing back.

Caoimhe followed him, concentrating on the placement of her feet in the dim light.

"You do love him, don't you?" murmured the harp under her arm.

"Aye."

"Do you fully know what this will mean for you?"

"What?"

"Becoming immortal. Living here in Faerie."

"I don't understand."

Uaithne sent a soft vibrating note into the night. "You will be wingless amongst the winged. You will have no magic amidst a people seeped in it. You will be alone in a multitude."

She sighed. "Yes, it will be difficult, but it will be worth it." Her eyes strayed to the slender Fae before her. "He is giving up a great deal for me as well."

The harp scoffed, "What is he losing?"

"He will be the object of ridicule and suspicion—I am no' so naïve as to think otherwise. He has been outcast by his family already. It will no' be easy."

"You are a strange being, little one."

Caoimhe shrugged. There was nothing more to say.

They moved onward in silence until she was so weary she thought she must rest or collapse where she stood. She no longer felt her feet. The rough path had numbed them.

Uaithne sang out with a discordant clash of strings.

Ailill turned, a frown marring his features. "What is it, harp?" he asked, his voice short with impatience.

"You forget yourself, hatchling. Your mortal here is fragile and tired. Sit for a few minutes, or you shall be carrying her ere long."

She heard the barely repressed sigh and cursed herself for her weakness. "I can go on," she protested, wincing as a particularly sharp stone broke through the numbness.

Ailill's countenance softened in the unnatural light. "No, he is right, beloved. I see it in your face. Here is a handy rock waiting to enthrone you," he smiled, taking her hand and leading her over to it. "We will sit a moment and rest. Are there any more of the *driw*? They have a property of refreshment to cure any fatigue."

She searched through the remnants of the food in her basket, finding two of the purple globes. She handed him one.

"Thank you, love," he murmured.

She bit into the juicy fruit and felt the sweet liquid run down her throat. Instantly she felt a surge of strength. Her heart lightened.

"Are you feeling any better?" she asked him softly.

"The pain is a dull ache now, constant and deep." His fingers strayed to his cheek. He shook his head. "What has she done?" he breathed.

"How much further to the keep?"

His head came up, eyes searching the horizon. "'Tis nearly dawn. We will be there ere mid-morning."

"That long?"

"Aye." His smile was bitter, and his eyes seemed to gaze at something far away. "'Tis the best we can do."

"Tell her the rest," admonished the harp.

Ailill started as if coming to himself. "There is nothing to tell."

"Secrets are no foundation to build a life on, hatchling."

Ailill flushed, the color surreal in the odd purplish light of the Faerie fire. He studied the ball of flame in his hand as if it fascinated him.

"Tell me what?" asked Caoimhe, her voice hushed.

"He could be there much faster alone."

"What do you mean?" she probed.

"Show her, Ailill Brightwing—if you care for your

sister, each moment is precious."

Ailill closed his eyes, swallowing hard. "You are right," he admitted at last. "It is the only way. You will see her safe to the keep?"

"Aye," promised the harp.

Ailill stood, carefully setting the ball of Faerie fire into a tiny hollow of the rock. "It will glow for a time untended," he said. "The sun should begin to rise ere it fades. Rest here until daybreak and then come after as quickly as able."

"Come after...?"

He took a deep breath then lifted his arms above his head. Throwing his head back, he dwindled to his flight stature, hovering in the air before her.

Her mouth dropped open. "True magic this," she whispered. "What other secrets are hidden from me?"

"I will tell you all in the centuries to come," promised the sprite, leaning in and placing a Faerie kiss on the tip of her nose. "Now, I must be off. There is little time. I must see the Dagda as soon as I may."

She waved him off. "Go on! I will follow."

He nodded and darted off into the night.

Caoimhe sighed. Suddenly the darkness seemed to press in hungrily around her. She hugged herself, rocking slightly as she sat on the rock.

"All will be well," soothed the harp. Softly, its strings began to sound.

Before she realized where she had heard the tune before, Caoimhe found herself curling up on the rock, eyes sleepily watching the flicker of the Faerie lantern. Within minutes, she was fast asleep.

Uaithne played on, keeping the night at bay.

Chapter Twenty-One

Aisling clung to Fergal, staring at Rhiannon aghast.

The Lady now wore a velvet riding habit as black as a moonless midnight. The ruby pendant about her neck glowed with an internal flame. Her flaxen braids had been gathered into an elaborate knot at the nape of her neck.

Looming behind her was a giant of a man in a cloak made from the hide of a full-grown stag. He wore the hollowed skull of the animal as a headdress, its horns brushing the ceiling of the tunnel. A huge brass horn hung at his hip.

Behind the pair, the tunnel was crowded with vague shapes and filled with sibilant whispers. The air stank of sulfur and unwashed flesh.

Aisling cringed instinctively against Fergal's chest, and his arms went around her in a protective circle.

"Isn't this sweet?" purred Rhiannon. "How touching. 'Tis too bad we don't have time for you to finish your reunion, my dear. The dawn comes apace, and I fear we must be about our business."

Aisling threw herself to her knees before Rhiannon's feet. "I beg you, Lady, spare Fergal from the Hunt. I will run before it in his place."

The Lady shook her head. "No, no. You do not understand. I look forward to this chase. We have not had so strong a quarry in far too long. He is a prize too great to relinquish easily."

"I'll give you anything you ask!"

Rhiannon's laugh was brittle as it rang from the walls of the tunnel. "My dear, you have nothing left to give. Unless you wish to offer up this mortal life you bargained so dearly for, I have all your treasures here." She lifted the ruby on her breast. "Your immortality, your beauty, your Fae magicks. There is nothing left for you to wager."

"Then give me a day—I beg you. Do no' do this thing tonight."

Rhiannon looked down at her through hooded eyes. Her mouth pursed in a moue of consideration. Finally, she sighed. "Oh, very well. You bargained fairly and gave much. I will grant you this one day. But tonight is the first of the full moon. We must hunt tomorrow. You will move me no further."

Aisling nodded miserably.

"You there." The Lady gestured imperiously to Fergal. "Help your lady into your chamber. She has won you one more sunrise. Use your time together wisely— but remember, tonight you run before the hounds. We don't want to be disappointed a second time because you are too exhausted to provide good sport."

Fergal picked Aisling up from the floor as if she were a child and carried her to the cell. "Thank you, my Lady," he murmured gravely.

Rhiannon rolled her eyes. "I am ever too soft-hearted," she replied with a huff of disgust.

Fergal nodded his head to the Lady as a one-legged creature hopped up to the door of the chamber. Its one eye blinked up at him balefully until he stepped into the cell with Aisling clutched to his chest.

The creature reached down with its one hand and

picked up the heavy latch beam as if it weighed a feather. It swung the door to with a clang.

Fergal heard the bar drop back into place across the doorway and then a soft heart-wrenching sob from the girl in his arms.

"Hush, sweetling," he murmured, dropping a kiss on her soft hair.

"Oh, Fergal...I've made such a mess of things."

"What do you mean, beloved?" he soothed, resting his chin atop her head.

"I should have come to her alone. Or made sure you were well away before I gave her my powers. I could have gotten you free of here if I were still Fae..." Her voice trailed away into muffled sobs.

"Come, now," he chided. "Be my brave girl."

He sat down on the edge of the rock bed he had been given, its hard surface softened only by a thin layer of straw. Rocking Aisling like a child, he whispered soothing nonsense until at last the sobs subsided into hitching gasps. "There...all better now?"

She straightened in his lap, gingerly brushing away the tears with the back of her hand as she sniffed and nodded.

One of the guttering torches cast its flickering glow about the cell, and he carefully took her chin in his hand, turning her head from side to side to examine the wounds. "Aisling, love—do you know what you've done to yourself?"

She nodded miserably. "I gave her my beauty in exchange for mortality." She gave a bitter little laugh. "Little chance I will have to regret one or enjoy the other."

He looked deep into her eyes. "There is a saying among the mortal folk—'while there is life, there is hope.' Do you understand what it means?"

"No' entirely."

"We haven't the centuries of time the Fae have to try and to fail. We have limited time upon this earth, but that doesn't mean we hold it any less dear. If anything, we value our short lives with greater jealously. We do no' easily give them up. We fight till the last breath for one more moment. Until the true, last breath comes and fades we believe there will be a next. We hope. I am no' giving up. We will find a way to cheat the Hunt— or die trying."

"That's what I am afraid of..." she sighed, "dying." She shuddered.

Fergal hugged her gently. "Do no' dwell on it, love. We have today. Let us make the best of it."

"What do you mean?"

"We can do nothing about the night until it comes, but we can enjoy this time we have been given." He tilted her head back and kissed her on each cheek, his lips feather-soft against the crusted wounds. "These are the most precious gifts anyone has ever offered me."

"You don't think I am hideous?" she whispered.

He shook his head. "Of course no'. How could I? You gave up—so much—for me. I am awed by your sacrifice."

She smiled wryly. "I would no' go so far."

"I would. To give up a future stretching to the ends of time and beauty to make the summer sun jealous..."

She giggled. "Now I know you are teasing me."

"Maybe a little," he admitted with a smile. "You are

still beautiful to me, Aisling. I will never see your face without remembering what you have given me."

She ducked her head shyly.

"Now, now, missy," he scolded with mock severity, tilting her head up. "Let me see you..." Suddenly, his eyes darkened, and he stopped mid-sentence. He set her on her feet. "Show me the rest," he ordered.

Aisling felt her heart skip a beat. "Must I?"

He nodded.

She turned away from him, presenting her back for his inspection.

She heard a deep groan and then felt gentle hands on her mangled flesh.

"My poor darling."

"It isn't so bad," she lied. "I hardly feel it any more."

"I don't believe that for a moment." He turned her to face him, gathering her into his arms. "I wish I could take away the pain."

"I will be fine."

"If only..."

"What?"

"Your poor back. I can't ask you to remove that dress. It's stuck to the wounds. There is water in the corner—" He gestured to a natural spring bubbling from the wall to fall into a stone basin on the floor and out again through a rock drain. "I could bath it free..."

"Why?"

He flushed. "I would like to see you without it," he mumbled. "At least once."

A sense of wonder filled her. "I would like that," she whispered, feeling the stir of emotions unfamiliar to her.

He still wore a tattered vest over his ragged shirt. Removing the outer garment, he stood and took her by the hand. Wordlessly, he led her to the spring.

He dipped the edge of the vest into the water, soaking the fabric. He rested the sodden bundle against her shoulder and squeezed water onto her ruined back.

The liquid was surprisingly warm. The outlet must be fed by a hot spring. The welcome warmth of the liquid soothed her wounded flesh.

He soaked the remnants of the spider gossamer and moonbeam fabric, and it dissolved beneath the water like the ethereal substance it was.

Aisling felt a sharp pang of regret. She would never weave the stuff of Faerie again. The whisper-soft fabric that felt light as air as it draped about the body...forever more a memory.

As the fabric washed away from the gashes, he continued gently sponging the crusted blood until the wounds were clean.

Aisling suddenly became conscious of the fact she had nothing else to wear. Nudity had never been a concern to her before, but now she felt unaccountably shy as she stood before Fergal.

She heard soft movement behind her, and then he turned her to face him.

He had removed his shirt and stood before her clad only in his ragged breeches.

She gazed at him in awe.

His chest was covered with a line of fine black hair that curled upon his breast. The muscles of his upper torso were well-defined, and his arms were corded from his labors.

She reached a tentative finger to touch the soft chest-hair. Fae folk grew no body hair. She laughed at the feel of it.

He reached out and cupped one of her small breasts in his hand.

She gasped at the spark that shot through her. What was happening to her?

He pulled her to him, conscious of her back.

The feel of his flesh on hers was almost too much to bear.

He bent down and captured her mouth with his own. His tongue nudged at her lip, and she opened for it, inviting its invasion.

Fergal pulled away with a ragged sigh. "I wish your back was no' so badly injured," he mumbled, his voice strangely tight.

"What do you mean?"

"I would show you—never mind."

Suddenly, she had a fairly good guess what he would show her. The thought excited her, sending a thrill up and down her spine.

"I think I could stand it," she murmured.

Fergal turned to her sharply, searching her face hungrily. "Are you sure you know what I—?"

"I believe so."

She smiled at him, moving to the edge of the stone cot and sitting upon it. The stone was chill under her buttocks. Taking a deep breath, she swung her legs up onto the rock and slowly lowered herself onto her back.

She stifled a gasp of pain. Nothing was going to take this from her. If she would be mortal for only one day, she would make the best of the precious day.

Fergal groaned and came to stand beside the stone. "Are you sure about this, Aisling? We could be looking for a way out of here—"

She shook her head. "There is no physical way out but the door, I promise you. However, there is a way out—in our minds—and I would very much like to explore it."

"Do you mean...?"

"Yes, please." She held up her arms, and he melted into them.

CHAPTER TWENTY-TWO

Ailill flew on through the darkness, his wings beating strong and sure. It felt good to soar through the dark, no matter what the reason. It was his normal mode of travel—to flit sprite-like, butterfly small from place to place. His time with Caoimhe had limited his flight, and he hadn't realized how much he resented the curtailment.

No, resented was the wrong word...regretted would be more apt. His heart lightened at the thought. He did not resent the constraints their relationship placed on him, with the future discontent they implied, but merely regretted the things he could not share with her. The difference boded well for their future together.

He scanned the horizon before him. It was still hours before dawn, but he did not need the Faerie flame to see his way. It had been one more concession to his mortal companion.

The thought gave him pause. Things would be this way for eternity. Even though she would be by his side as an immortal, Caoimhe would not obtain the other gifts of Faerie. They would never fly together through a moonlight night, playing tag with the fireflies. They would never dive into a midnight pool and swim through the cool darkness without need of light. There would never be a nest with a rainbow-tinted egg shivering into a three-inch hatchling, all gangling wings and appetite.

This was the first time he had allowed himself to

speculate in that direction. What *might* be possible? He'd heard whispers of children with mixed parentage—usually a Fae father and a mortal mother—but he'd never actually seen one.

Would he be able to give Caoimhe a child? She deserved one. If he could not, he should tell her and let her go back to her people. Something could be worked out...the rules of Faerie could be bent further than he'd led her to believe. He was sure the Dagda could send her back to her life with little if any remembrance of her time with the Sidhe...but he did not want it to end there. He wanted to keep her by his side for all time.

The Dagda would know. Avallach was King. He knew everything.

Ailill looked up in surprise. He was already back to the keep. It was amazing how much faster the journey took with wings. He would never take them for granted again!

Suddenly, a realization crashed home for him with such force that he fell from the sky to the silky lawn. He lay facedown in the tall grass, breathing in the scent of life as his mind whirled dizzily. Wings.

He knew now what was wrong with Aisling. The dull ache along his back throbbed, as if to say "clever boy."

Aisling had been stripped of her wings. She was no longer Fae.

* * *

It was several hours before he could get an audience before the Dagda. Ailill chafed at the delay. When at last he was shown into the throne room by a less-than-gracious aide de camp, he was about ready to explode.

"My Lord Avallach," he began.

"Did you bring my harp?"

The question threw him off balance. It was the least of his worries at the moment. He had completely forgotten it would be the only thing Avallach wanted from him.

"It is on its way. I came ahead."

"You what?" The Dagda's voice grew sharp, and his brow clouded with anger.

"I came ahead. Caoimhe is bringing Uaithne with her."

"And exactly why did you leave my most precious possession with a mortal female?"

It was on the tip of his tongue to reply, "*And exactly why did you bet your most precious possession in the first place?*" but he bit back the urge. "I had to get to you quickly, and she could no' fly."

"What was so urgent?"

Now that the question was asked, he felt a fool. What could he say—"my sister is in trouble?" How would he know? Not everyone believed in the connection between twins, and fewer still understood the depths it could boast.

Ailill took a deep breath. He had to try. "It is Aisling, lord. She has gotten herself into serious trouble."

"What do you mean?"

"I feel it. She has lost her wings."

The Dagda scoffed. "Impossible."

"I know how it sounds, Lord, but I—"

The door to the chamber opened, and Ailill turned. Caoimhe came into the throne room, Uaithne cradled in her arms. His heart rose at the mere sight of her.

She came forward tentatively and set the instrument

on the foot of the dais. With a bobbed curtsey, she stepped back beside Ailill.

The Dagda reached down and caressed the top of the harp. "So, you have fulfilled your part of the bargain. I will do the same."

He called in the guard from the hallway. "Bring me a golden apple from the Eternal Tree," he ordered.

"As you command," murmured the guard with a bow. His glance raked over Caoimhe, and his lip curled contemptuously.

A fiery color spread up her pale cheeks, but she continued to stare straight ahead. Ailill reached over and took her hand, giving it a squeeze of comfort.

"Now. Before you arrived, my dear," the Dagda said to Caoimhe, "Ailill was telling me a most interesting story..."

"It is no' a story! Aisling is in trouble."

"He says his sister has lost her wings. Where would he get such a foolish idea?"

"I do no' know, my Lord. I have never seen his sister...though she was with him in the market the day we met. They had separated to pursue their own interests..."

"In other words, he stormed off in a huff, no?"

"I was no' there, my Lord. I cannot say."

Avallach turned to Ailill. "She is a good consort for you, rash one. She tells me truth without blackening your reputation. You could have done much worse in choosing a life-mate."

"I think so, lord," Ailill replied, gazing down at her with a smile.

"However," continued the Dagda, "I still do not know why you are so certain your sister is in trouble.

Simply leaving her at the mortal Faire—"

"—She had met a man."

"Ah...the plot thickens. So, you brought your mortal here, and fear she has decided to stay there with hers?"

"Aye, lord."

Avallach nodded gravely. "I see. Such a circumstance *could* lead to the loss of her wings. My own brother renounced his Fae heritage for the sake of a pretty face." He was silent a moment, lost in thought, then continued once more, "There is only one place to go if you wish to give up all that is Fae and become a mortal—the throne room of the White Lady, Rhiannon of the Unseelie Court. Her magic is dark where ours is light. The Unseelie mock all that is Sidhe, despite being a part of it. If Aisling has lost her wings, she will have done so there." The King paused for effect. "But hear me, lad. No one who goes to the White Lady's dark place returns unscathed. It is better to forget and continue with your own life. You have won immortality for your bride. Enjoy it. Get to know one another. Let your life begin here."

"I cannot abandon Aisling. We are twins. Halves of the same whole. How can I forget her?"

"If you are determined to save her, you will have to go to the Unseelie Kingdom. Will you go alone? Your beloved here may become immortal, but she will never be Fae. She will not be able to fly at your side. And it is the only way to reach the Court in time."

"In time for what?"

"The Wild Hunt will ride tonight. My spies told me it was delayed for a whim of the Lady, but she must ride tonight. The moon is full, and her power will wane with it if she does not hold the Hunt. Rhiannon would never let that happen."

"How can you be sure?"

"She is my daughter. I know her mind, even if she chooses to distance herself from her heritage."

"Is there nothing to do then?"

"I tell you what...I like you, lad. You amuse me. I will lend you a pair of my horses so you and your lady may ride. Their gait is like the wind. Go to Rhiannon. Perhaps she will listen to your pleas."

There was a light rap upon the door, and Avallach called for the visitor to enter. The guard who had been to the orchard came forward, an apple sitting in the midst of a white linen napkin upon a golden tray. He came to the foot of the throne and bowed.

The Dagda gestured Caoimhe forward. "Here is your reward, my dear. Take it, and eat. You will gain your immortality."

Caoimhe glanced sideways at Ailill's pale set countenance. This was her chance to be with him for eternity. Would he grow weary of her? Would he regret not having a consort to fly amongst the stars beside him?

He turned toward her. "Please, beloved. Eat."

She stepped forward and took the apple into her hand. It shone like solid gold but was slightly warm from its day spent in the orchard. It was difficult to convince herself the apple was flesh and would not break her teeth if she bit it, so she closed her eyes.

With a mental farewell to the world she knew, she bit into the apple. The fruit was crisp and delightfully cool on her tongue. She felt a rush of energy and an uplift to her spirits. It was the most delicious taste she had ever experienced—nothing like an apple from the village orchard. She ate it quickly, not wanting to delay Ailill further than necessary.

"There, it is done," murmured Avallach, clapping his hands.

Caoimhe opened her eyes slowly. There was a new sharpness to her sight, bringing everything into a hyper-focus. The colors of the room were enhanced to almost painful brilliance. "Ohhh..." she breathed.

The Dagda laughed at her wonder. "It will take some getting used to, my dear. But now, for better or worse, you are immortal. Barring traumatic injury or deliberate action on the part of a villain, you and your Ailill will have eternity to spend together. May you be forever blessed."

"Thank you, my Lord," she murmured, sinking into a full curtsey.

"Get up, little one," he scolded. "There is no need for such formality." He turned to Ailill. "As for you, my lad...if you are determined to your course, I will have horses saddled and brought to the gate. You must hurry though. The sun shall set anon, and if you are not there before the Hunt begins, it will be too late."

Chapter Twenty-Three

Afterwards, Aisling lay in Fergal's arms, content to be there, despite what the future might hold. She might die tonight, but at least she had lived. Emotions ran rampant in her heart. She had never felt anything so vividly, so completely, before. She had noticed her senses were no longer as sharp as they had been when she was Fae, but her *feelings*, her emotions, were hyper-sensitive.

She traced a finger through the thick hair on Fergal's chest and sighed happily.

"What is it, beloved?" he asked softly.

She could feel the rumble of his voice under her hand and nearly laughed aloud. "Nothing. I just feel so...content...and happy."

"In the midst of all this, you can still feel happy?" he teased.

"Aye. With you at my side."

His face grew grave. "Will it be enough for you, Aisling? Can you really be content as the wife of a village tanner? Living in one room behind the shop? Growing old and gray as time goes on?"

"It sounds wonderful to me, my love."

He kissed her.

His hand began to roam about her body again, stirring up more of those wonderful sensations that caused her to moan with the pleasure. Before he could pursue the matter further, however, there was a scratching on the door of the cell.

They sat up abruptly. As he scrambled for his trousers and shirt Fergal called out, "What do you want? Who is there?"

He tossed the shirt to Aisling and then drew on his trousers.

Aisling slipped on the tattered shirt, wincing as the rough fabric contacted her sore back.

They heard the bar draw back, and the door opened a crack. The gwyllion peeked her tousled head around the edge of the door. "Thought the foolish one might need this," she mumbled, tossing something into the cell. "I'll try to bring food. You will need your strength."

Aisling climbed stiffly off the slab of rock and retrieved the cloth from the floor. It was a dress made of some silky fabric, cool and slippery as water in her hands.

"It will chafe the wounds less than the coarse thing you wear," commented the gwyllion. "I will go now. If I am no' back before the Lady comes—take care. Remember, the Hounds can smell better than they can see..."

And she was gone as quickly as she had come.

Aisling gave Fergal back his shirt and drew the silky cloth of the sheath over her head. It did feel good against her back. The smooth surface glided over the wounds instead of catching on them as the shirt had done.

"You are beautiful, my love," murmured Fergal softly.

She moved back to the rock, perching on the edge of it with one foot tucked beneath her. "What of you, Fergal O'Connor, will you be content with a wife who knows nothing of cooking or housework? Who has fanciful ideas and foolish ways?"

He kissed the tip of her nose. "Who has sacrificed family, friends, and Faerie magicks to be at my side? I only hope I will prove worthy of her."

Aisling felt her cheeks grow hot. "And I of you, my Lord." She sighed, resting her head upon his shoulder. "But it will no' matter, will it? No one escapes the Wild Hunt. If only..."

"If only what, my love?"

"I would have liked to say good-bye to Ailill. He didn't understand why I wanted to stay with you in the village—but if I could only talk to him...tell him how happy I am."

"You can tell him when you see him next."

She shook her head. "I'm no' likely to see him again. Even if we survive the Hunt, he is Fae, and now, I am no'."

"He is still your brother. The ties of blood are thicker than any other alliance."

"Perhaps you are right," she murmured, though privately she doubted her twin would see it the same way.

"We will escape this place, Aisling, and when we do, I will take you to the gates of Faerie if you wish it."

"We will see," she replied evasively, smiling at his willingness to please her.

"I have a plan," promised Fergal. "When the creature returns, we will overpower it before it can sound an alarm. If we can get out into the tunnels, it will be a simple matter of eluding the Lady's minions long enough to make our way to the surface."

Aisling didn't see anything simple in the least about the plan.

"You won't hurt her, will you?" she asked anxiously. "She has been kind to me."

"I promise," soothed Fergal. "I will be careful."

The telltale scratching sounded at the door once

more, and Fergal went quickly to stand behind the portal. When the door creaked open, and the gwyllion poked her head around the edge of it, Fergal grabbed her about the neck.

The creature squeaked, dropping the fruit and bread it carried to spill in a wide arc on the floor. Aisling hurried to pick up the food and wrap it in the remains of Fergal's vest.

Fergal held the gwyllion by the back of the neck, lifting it off its feet. It kicked and squirmed in his grip.

Aisling rushed to them. "Hush, please," she begged Gwyllion. "He will no' harm you. He promised." She leveled a stern glance at Fergal. "Put her down now."

Fergal started to protest then shrugged, setting the little creature gently on its feet.

"We need to get out of here before the Hunt," Aisling told the gwyllion. "Can you help us?"

"'Tis more than my life is worth to do so!" protested Gwyllion. "The Lady will kill me for it."

"Then don't help us, but don't hinder either. Stay here in the cell. You can say Fergal overpowered you, and we forced our way out."

"Him? Overpower me?" snorted the creature. "No' like!"

Fergal smirked. "'Twould be easy enough, little one." He reached for its arm.

The gwyllion sidestepped his reach and grabbed his wrist. It flipped him onto the floor and sat on his chest. "So easy?"

Fergal grimaced. "No' so easy, I concede."

"Get up off of him, Gwyllion. We have no time to waste," scolded Aisling, though she was secretly amused.

The little mountain Fae complied. "I will tell you this much," she commented. "If you follow the tunnel out of here it will branch to left and right. Take the left fork. Go left when it branches three times, and then go right. You will come out at the surface. Hurry. It grows late."

Aisling hugged her impulsively. "Thank you, Gwyllion."

"Shuri," the gwyllion shyly whispered in her ear. "My name is Shuri."

Aisling stiffened, realizing the significance of the gift. "I will keep it safe," she promised softly.

"Come, Aisling," urged Fergal. "There is no time to waste."

"I'm coming," she called. The last sight she had of Shuri was a glimpse of the little gwyllion sitting on the rock slab hugging her knees to her chest.

They went swiftly through the dim passage to the first fork. Aisling tied her food bundle securely and slung it around her waist to free her hands for clambering over the rocks that partially blocked the passage in places.

They took the first left-hand tunnel, heartened to see the floor sloping upward beneath their feet. Aisling's long sheath-like dress caught on the rock walls several times before Fergal made her stop and rip off the bottom of it.

The going was smoother afterwards, and they soon came to a second fork in the path. The left passage wound up out of sight, and they hurried along it. The air was getting noticeably cooler, even though the pair had several twistings yet to go.

Aisling dared to let hope creep into her heart. They would be free! The Hunt would not rend them limb from limb.

They reached the third fork and again went left. It felt like they had been climbing for hours, and Aisling's legs trembled with the effort of keeping up with Fergal's longer strides. She fell further and further behind, despite her best intentions.

Finally, Fergal turned and noticed she was some distance behind. He hurried back to her. "We'll rest for a minute, beloved. Here. Sit on this rock and eat something."

Aisling allowed him to ease her down onto a boulder. Gratefully, she plucked a soft roll from her bundle and split it down the middle. "Take this," she urged. "You need to keep up your strength as well."

They ate the bread in silence, both wrapped up in their private thoughts. Too soon, the respite was over. Fergal sighed and took her hand. "Come, love. We must be clear of the tunnel before they come to fetch us."

Aisling nodded. "Aye."

There was a tantalizing breeze winding through the tunnels now, bringing with it a breath of fresh air and the scent of living growth. They began to talk of inconsequential things, secure in their escape.

Fergal told Aisling of his childhood, bringing giggles bubbling out of her in response to his adventures. In turn, she regaled him with stories of the hatchlings and the beauties of Faerie.

Soon, they came to the fourth branching of the path. Fergal moved toward the entrance to the right-hand tunnel. Aisling hung back, shaking her head.

"Come on," he said impatiently. "This is the way out."

"I don't think so," she replied, her voice timid yet determined.

"She said three lefts and then right."

"No, she said 'take the left fork. Go left when it branches three times, and *then* go right.'"

"That's what I said. This is the fork we are supposed to turn right."

"No, Fergal. We are to go left three times after the first tunnel, then right."

He sighed in exasperation. "Aisling, I can feel the stir of air. It is stronger here on the right. You misunderstood her, 'tis all. Come on. We are almost free!"

Aisling knew in her heart he was mistaken. They should take the left fork...but he was so sure he was right. "As you say, Fergal," she whispered, allowing him to pull her forward along the right-hand tunnel.

They were almost running by the time they reached the end of the passageway. It had climbed steadily upward the whole time, and Aisling had to admit the air was fresher and cooler along *this* corridor. Rounding one last boulder, they burst into open air.

"Well, well, well. Isn't this wonderful, Herne? We don't have to fetch our quarry after all."

Aisling realized with a sinking heart they had emerged from the tunnel into the kennel of the Hounds.

Chapter Twenty-Four

Ailill and Caoimhe rode like the wind on a pair of matched white horses with manes and tails of gold. She had never ridden anything more spirited than her father's overweight plow horse, but somehow she felt as if she belonged in the saddle. Both Ailill and the Dagda had assured her the horse would bear her safely, so she rode without a second thought.

They flew over the countryside—if not literally, as close as may be. Neither spoke. It would take too much precious energy to speak above the rush of wind. They silently agreed to conserve their resources for what was to come.

When they had come out of the Faerie hill, they found the sun halfway to the west. It was a disorienting moment before Caoimhe remembered that in the mortal realm, this was nearly sunset instead of shortly after dawn. Already she had begun to think of things in Faerie as the normal state of being.

Ailill had told her the Unseelie Court was not housed in a Fae dimension. They preferred to have their barrow in the mortal realm with the humans they considered their playthings. When the sun sank behind the western horizon, 'twould be time for the Hunt to begin.

The horses pounded tirelessly through the late afternoon, but Caoimhe's slight body was beginning to feel as if every bone had been bruised then liquefied by the ride.

"Please, Ailill," she called when she could stand no more. "Can we rest for a wee moment?"

Ailill cast a glance over at the westering sun. "For a moment, then," he agreed reluctantly, reining in his stallion. "Only a moment."

Caoimhe slid from the mare's back with a groan. There was a stream beside the path, and she stooped to bathe her face in the cool water.

Ailill leapt lightly down from the horse and joined her beside the stream. He scooped up a handful of the chilled water and drank from his cupped hands.

"Will we be in time?" she asked him gravely.

"We have to be," he answered. "I am determined to stop the Hunt. Or, at the very least, to rescue my sister and Fergal O'Connor from the Unseelie band."

"Fergal O'Connor? What has he to do with this?" Caoimhe questioned, surprised to hear his name in the context.

"Fergal O'Connor is the mortal my fool sister fancies herself in love with."

Caoimhe felt a rush of sympathy for the girl she had never met. "Why call you Aisling a fool, Ailill Brightwing? Because she loves a mortal? Surely no self-respecting Fae would do so!"

He flushed, telling her the barb had hit home. "I see what you are saying, love..."

"It is somehow fitting for it be Fergal," she continued thoughtfully, relenting almost at once. "He is a good man. I can see why she would abandon Faerie for a man such as Fergal."

"You talk as if you know him well."

"Aye. We grew up together. His grandfather, Seamus, has approached my father for my hand in marriage, and they were beginning to work out details.

Neither of us was particularly interested in the match, but 'twasn't seen as a problem by our elders. It is nice to know we will both be happy with someone we can truly love, instead of trying to pretend for the sake of our relatives."

Ailill swept her into his arms and kissed her soundly. "You definitely are no longer available for a marriage arrangement," he declared. "You are stuck with me for all time."

"Let's hope you don't come to regret it," she teased.

"No' in a million years. But come, it is time we were moving on." He cast a glance at the sun. "'Tis getting late."

"Aye," she agreed with a nod. "We must be on time, Ailill."

They mounted their horses and rode on through the rioting colors of sunset. The desolate moor was awash with orange and crimson light. But even the warmth of the setting sun could not bring life to the windswept landscape they approached. Stunted gorse bushes and close-growing peat were the only life growing in this lonely place.

Caoimhe shivered. After being a guest of Faerie, limited though her time had been there, the aching loneliness hit home all the harder.

Ailill rode as if he knew where he was bound, and she wondered at his certainty. How did he know where the Unseelie would hold their Hunt? Was it common knowledge amongst the Seelie Court, or had he secret information won by guile and stealth?

The setting sun shone directly in her eyes now, and she raised a hand to shade them. The land was gently rolling hillocks as far as she could see, like a frozen seascape...but in the distance—at the far edge of the horizon rose a lonely tor.

Ailill pointed at the crag. "There is where we journey. The Unseelie band make their home beneath that rock. We will find the Hunt somewhere close by, I am sure. If Aisling is as injured as I fear, she will no' be in any shape for long distance running. We must look sharp. When the moon rises, the Hunt will begin. If we have no' found them before the hounds set forth, we will have little chance of saving them."

She nodded. They would be on time. There was no other option. She would not lose the sister she had yet to meet to the ravening jaws of the Wild Hounds.

Ailill would never forgive himself if he were unable to rescue Aisling. He felt responsible for abandoning her in the village. If they could not save her, he would be a broken man.

And Fergal had gifted her with her first kiss. It had been behind the mill in the shadow of the great wheel. She remembered it as if it were yesterday.

No, they would not fail. They would be on time!

The big white horses strode on, in perfect rhythm. Matching stride for stride, they had the smoothest gait she had ever felt. She could get used to such a ride. After her bruises were gone, of course.

The last edge of the sun slipped behind the horizon, leaving the world mauve and gray. It was so quiet and still she almost fancied they were the last beings left alive...until a raven circled overhead with a high-pitched caw.

She saw Ailill glance sharply up at the bird, but she could not tell if it were in dismay or surprise. The odd gray-purple color of the light caused shapes to flatten, making it difficult to determine details of land or beast, friend or foe.

Soon, even that dim light faded into obscurity. She gave the mare her head and prayed the horse could see better than she could.

"Look," Ailill cried, pointing to the horizon. The moon was lifting like a big orange lantern. It was a perfect circle of light cut out of the night sky.

"The Hunt begins anon. As soon as the moon rises enough to see by, they will ride. We must find the others now."

"Where do we look?" asked Caoimhe, overwhelmed by a sense of hopelessness. The moor stretched for miles in every direction. How could they guess where to look for the pair before the Hunt began?

"Follow my lead," Ailill ordered, turning the stallion away from the smooth path they had been following and onto the uneven surface of the moor. "We have a guide."

"What?"

"Do you no' see it?" He pointed upward, his arm a dim shape in the gloom. "The raven."

"I can't see a thing," she replied, shaking her head.

"Trust me. It is there."

"Lead on. I will follow."

He galloped off across the moor as if it were bright noon. She took a deep breath and willed the mare to be careful. It was not her wish to spend eternity as Ailill's crippled husk of a wife.

The animals appeared to share Ailill's keen vision. They raced on with no trace of hesitation.

The pounding sound of the hooves was soothing, and Caoimhe caught her head nodding. How she could even contemplate sleep at a time like this was beyond her, but a near fall from the horse was enough to raise her adrenaline and erase the last trace of fatigue. Heart pounding, she held on more tightly and paid attention to where they ran.

The moon was now more golden than orange. It was shrinking, as if distancing itself from the proceedings below, mayhap wanting no part in the game set to begin.

Ailill still held a straight course across the moor. She could not see the bird he claimed to be following, but everything else looked like silver cutouts against black paper. The eerie moonlight flattened the landscape to two dimensions, and she felt dizzy trying to make sense of the scene.

A wavering howl sounded somewhere in front of them, followed by the blast of a horn blowing loud and shrill.

"It begins!" Ailill cried. "The Hunt goes forth. We must hurry!" He leaned over his horse's neck and urged it to go faster and more.

Caoimhe held her breath, terrified by the speed at which they sailed over the ground. She was not as confident a rider as he.

The moon was now its familiar cold self, pale and aloof.

Her gaze darted from side to side, searching the inkblot landscape for any trace of movement. They had to be on time!

"There," Ailill cried, pointing into the distance. "Do you see them?"

She did see a flash of movement, a pale shape on the horizon. "Yes, I see."

A swell of relief flowed through her. They would do it. They would be able to rescue Aisling and Fergal from the terror of the Hunt.

"You take Aisling," Ailill ordered. "I'll get Fergal." He veered his horse slightly left.

Nodding, though she knew he wasn't watching, Caoimhe peered through the darkness, searching for the pale flash of movement she had glimpsed a moment before.

There! The girl was there!

Bending down precariously, she held out her hand. "Give me your hand," she cried, as she rode up beside the stumbling runner. "Hurry! There is no time!"

Chapter Twenty-Five

Rhiannon was dressed once more in the black velvet habit, a wickedly barbed riding crop in one hand. Her excitement was palpable as she played idly with the tip of the whip.

Herne the Hunter loomed behind her in his horned headdress, a cruel smile of anticipation crooking his lips. One hand was hooked around the collar of a huge black hound that strained eagerly toward the pair standing frozen in the mouth of the tunnel.

Smaller hounds, coats darker than midnight, were held in check by bogles with grinning mouths full of sharp teeth splitting their goblin faces. They chittered excitedly when they saw their quarry, bouncing on their toes in their eagerness.

Aisling hid her face against Fergal's chest. It was all for naught. They had escaped nothing. They had merely saved Rhiannon the trouble of fetching them.

His arms came around her for what little comfort he could offer. It was a crushing blow.

"Very touching," the Lady said with a yawn that belied the words. "Well, shall we get started then? The sun is about to set. In the interest of sport, we will give you until an hour after moonrise to get as far away as you can."

She tossed a pair of worn boots at Aisling's feet. "Here. Wouldn't want you to be slowed down by the fact you can no longer transform and fly. There is no entertainment in a hunt with no room for surprises.

If you can manage to elude us until the moon sets, we will concede the hunt, and you are both free to return to whatever little lives you have planned. Any and all methods of chase are allowed, as are all possible means of escape. There are no further rules. No quarter is asked, and none will be given. If we catch you, you are ours to do with as we see fit. Any questions?"

Wordlessly, Fergal shook his head. He bent to help Aisling into the boots, disheartened by her dull eyes and slumped posture. "All will be well," he whispered against her hair as he stood. "We *will* survive."

"How?" she sobbed, the word catching in her throat.

He took her hand. "I don't know," he admitted softly, "but we can't give up. Remember hope? Hope is all we have."

She sniffed back tears and nodded, a brave smile on her face. "You're right. We aren't done for yet."

"Are you two through?" broke in Rhiannon with an exasperated sigh. "It is time."

She snapped her fingers, and a break appeared in the circle of creatures. "Go! You are wasting your grace and trying my patience."

Fergal led Aisling from the circle into the open moor beyond. He glanced back over his shoulder, and the Unseelie enclave was gone. All he could see was a tumble of boulders at the bottom of a high tor.

For an instant, he let himself believe it was all a nightmare. There was no Wild Hunt. There were no wicked hunters with fangs and claws as deadly as their hounds.

Then a high wavering howl rose on the suddenly keening wind, and he knew it was no dream. 'Twas a living nightmare.

"Come, love," he urged. "We must put as much distance between us as we can."

Aisling nodded.

He glanced around him swiftly, trying to get his bearings in country he had only seen upside-down from the perspective of Jack-In-Irons' back. "I think there is a stream this way—it might help hide our tracks."

"We must be wary of the water, love. There are wicked things in the depths and creatures that would just as gladly rip you to pieces as the Hounds themselves," Aisling warned.

"It is all I can think to do," he countered. "If we can break our scent..."

She held her tongue, but silently thought the possibility of hiding their scent from Rhiannon's hounds was slight at best. "As you say, love."

They struggled forward, hampered by Aisling's boots—which proved too large—and flimsy dress. The silky fabric caught in every bush they passed.

Fergal seethed in impatience. They were leaving a trail a blind man could follow. Finally, he stopped her and ripped the dress away until it hung in a ragged edge an inch above her knees. "There. 'Tis less likely to slow us down further," he promised, glancing at the tiny edge of sun remaining about the horizon. "We should make better time now. We have to cover more ground before the moon rises."

They found the stream he remembered and splashed through it to the other side. After a few hundred feet, they crossed it again, returning to their original bank. They made several of these jags, hoping to confuse their scent.

Aisling stumbled along behind him, unused to so much ground travel. She could have flown the same distance in moments if she had ever had a mind, but the pace Fergal set was pushing her to exhaust what little strength she had left. Still, she pressed gamely on until she tripped over a clump of grasses and went down in a heap. She bit her lip, determined not to weep, even as her slim ankle began to swell inside the boot.

Fergal was nearly out of sight in the dim twilight before he realized she wasn't with him and called out softly. "Aisling? Where are you?"

"Here," she moaned, rocking against the pain in her ankle. "I-I don't know if I can go on."

He knelt beside her, removing her boot and squinting down at her ankle in the growing darkness. "It looks a bit swollen. Let's see what we can do to fix that."

She could hear the note of false jollity he interjected into his voice and tried not to lose heart. "Is it very bad?"

"No, merely a slight sprain. Do you still have the bundle of food?"

"Yes," she replied meekly. "Though I think I've lost part of it on the road."

"No matter," he soothed. "'Tis the cloth I need now. Might as well eat up the fruit and bread for strength while I tear the vest for bindings."

She nodded her understanding and separated the meager foodstuffs into two piles. Each of them got a roll and a wizened apple. It wasn't much, but it was better than no food at all. After she had everything out of the bundle, she handed him the cloth, and he tore it into bandages.

Taking her ankle in hand, he bound the ankle tightly and slipped her boot back on her foot. "It won't be easy, but we have to go on, Aisling." He pointed to the horizon.

The moon was rising like a glowing orange. "We only get another hour's head start."

"If she told the truth," Aisling murmured. "I do no' trust her to keep her word."

"All the more reason we must hurry." He rose to his feet and reached down a hand to her. "Come, love."

"You should go on without me," she commented. "I will only slow you down. You could be free without me."

"After all we've gone through? No, beloved. If one of us falls to the Hunt, we both do. But I am no' yet ready to give up the fight." He grabbed her wrist and lifted her up. "If I have to sling you across my back and carry you, I shall, but I must warn you—it is a deucedly uncomfortable way to travel. I speak from experience."

She giggled a little at his foolishness, and her spirits lifted a mite. "All right. I'll try."

Slowly and painfully, they continued on their way.

Fergal kept one eye on the rising moon. Soon its color faded from orange to pale gold and then to the creamy pearl he was used to. It had been at least an hour since moonrise. The Hunt would be after them soon.

As if in answer to the thought, there was a high, keening howl in the distance behind them, and the reedy blare of a far distant horn blowing a call to the Hunt.

Aisling froze. "They are coming!" she whispered.

"Aye, so we had best run," he answered grimly. "Forget your ankle and run as fast as you may. It is our only hope."

She nodded, clutching his hand hard enough to grind the bones.

Fergal ignored the pain and squeezed back reassuringly. "You can do it, love. We will beat her."

Aisling tried to smile, but the effort only produced a grimace. "I am ready."

The horn sounded again, impossibly nearer. They began to run.

Aisling fought to keep up with Fergal, every step an agony. She ran for all she was worth, her breath coming in ragged gasps.

The horn sounded again, and this time it seemed to come from in front of them. Fergal changed direction without breaking stride, angling off perpendicular to their course.

Aisling turned to follow and came down hard on her bad ankle. Choking back a cry of pain, she stumbled on. It was getting harder and harder to keep her footing. But she had no choice.

There were baying hounds on the wind now, and they seemed to surround the fleeing couple. She could make out the sounds of shouts carrying back and forth between riders. The horn rang almost continuously.

The landscape was an ink and ivory woodcut. Shadows seemed to spring out of nowhere, and Aisling was terrified the next one would be a slavering hound ready to rip her throat out.

Fergal ran easily, with huge ground-eating strides that seemed to melt the distance. He had a dancer's grace and an athlete's stamina.

Struggle as she might, Aisling could not keep up with him. She was falling further and further behind, and the hounds were closing. She forced herself to go faster. She could not bear the thought of falling to the hounds.

At the sound of galloping hooves behind her, Aisling screamed, a high-pitched wail of loss and despair.

"Give me your hand," cried an unfamiliar female voice, and she glanced up to see a huge white horse bearing down on her. The rider, a mortal girl whose hair shone pale in the moonlight, was reaching out to her. "Hurry! There's no time!"

She could see a second horse galloping behind Fergal, and the rider was Fae. She would recognize that silhouette in the darkest night. She knew it as well as her own.

Without a second thought, she reached up and grabbed the girl's hand. The stranger swung her off her feet, and Aisling thought her arm would pull from its socket before she managed to grab a handful of mane and haul herself up onto the horse in front of the unknown rider.

"Got her!" called her rescuer.

Aisling saw the other rider nod and reach down for Fergal's hand.

Fergal swung onto the galloping horse as if he did so every day before breakfast.

A whooping cry of triumph split the night, and Aisling's identification of the other rider was confirmed.

Ailill had come to their rescue. But who was this girl, and how had they known where to find them?

"I'm sure you have questions, Lady," the girl shouted against the wind—almost as if she had read her thoughts—then continued, "but they will have to wait. We are no' free of the Hunt yet. We must ride before the Hounds until dawn, or they will kill us all."

Chapter Twenty-Six

Aisling clung to the horse's mane, dizzy with relief. It was a miracle—the arrival of rescue out of the night—unexpected and oh, so welcome. She searched for the other horse until she saw it, glowing in the moonlight ahead.

"Hang on," the girl behind her warned. "If we don't outride them, we're done for."

Aisling nodded and tightened her grip on the mane. The night was chill, and the speed of the horse made the wind whip past her. She shivered in the light dress Shuri had given her. Especially since she'd lost the bottom third of it.

"We'll get you somewhere warm as soon as we may," promised the stranger behind her. "Ailill was planning to turn back toward Faerie soon."

"But I can't go there," Aisling murmured automatically. "I am no longer Fae."

"Aye," acknowledged her companion, "but the Dagda has power against the Unseelie to make them stay their hands before they get too close."

Aisling felt her head swimming. Who *was* this mortal, and how did she know so much about the Fae?

"All will be explained." Again, it was as if the girl read her mind. The thought was not a pleasant one.

They could hear the hounds baying behind them and angry shouts and catcalls. The horn rang through the night as Herne tried to rally his riders. But, in the end, it was to no avail.

The Dagda's horses were like no others. Swift and tireless, they carried the companions through the night, gradually out-distancing the Hunt and leaving the Unseelie Court far behind.

Still, they didn't slow until they reached the outskirts of the tiny village where the entire adventure had begun. It had been the Dagda's idea. Since they were a mixed band of mortal and Fae, there was only one logical place to go, and he had recommended Ailill take his companions directly there.

They drew to a stop before Tadhg's imposing dwelling, and all but Aisling slid boneless from the saddle. Fergal came around and lifted her from the mare, refusing to put her down.

"You've done enough damage to your ankle as it is," he scolded. "I will no' have you lamed for life."

She giggled weakly. "I am no' so easily damaged, my Lord. I am perfectly fit to walk."

"You've been through enough," he murmured, shaking his head, eyes shadowed. "You must rest now."

"Yes, my Lord," she sighed in mock exasperation, laying her head against his muscled chest.

Ailill stepped quickly to the door and rapped upon it. He was the one most out of place if they were caught out, and he did not intend to be an exhibit in someone's traveling show.

The door opened at once, and Tadhg gestured them inside hurriedly, as if expecting them.

"Put her here, Fergal," he ordered, gesturing to a soft chair before a crackling fire. "There is a stool there—slide it gently under her foot. Tsk, tsk, little one. You've gone and gotten yourself in terrible shape."

Ailill caught his first clear look at Aisling and stifled a cry of horror. "What have you done, Aisling?"

Her hands flew self-consciously to her wounded cheeks. "I-I...oh, Ailill—I thought you would understand." She hid her face in her hands; great wracking sobs shook her slender shoulders.

He went and knelt beside her chair, taking her hands in his and pulling them away from her face. "Oh, love. I *do* understand. You found something you never bargained for at the Faire. So did I." He let go one of her hands and reached his out to Caoimhe.

Shyly, she took it and let herself be pulled forward.

"This is Caoimhe Sinclair. She will be coming back with me to Faerie. Father does no' approve, but the Dagda has promised us a corner where we can build a home and raise a garden in return for tending his horses. He gave my Caoimhe an apple with his own hand, he did. So you see, you may be leaving Faerie for Fergal, but I am taking home a mortal bride. Life is strange, is it no'?"

Fergal held his arms out to Caoimhe. "Congratulations, dear friend. I am glad you have found someone to make you happy. I know I would no' have been the one."

Caoimhe smiled at him fondly. "And I am happy for you as well, Fergal O'Connor. You have found a lovely lady of your own. And we shall be family nonetheless."

"True," he laughed. "Though who would believe? And as you stay young and beautiful, will you remember those of us who are poor mortals?"

"Aye," she said with a stern glower. "The Dagda said 'tis the mortal realm who shall forget *me* as I live among the Fae."

"True enough," nodded Tadhg. "The world will begin to forget a mortal who has found a home with the Fae...just as the Fae forget a former comrade who has renounced his wings." He sighed. "As my own brother forgets I exist unless he needs a favor in the middle of the night."

A merry smile replaced his theatrical frown. "But it is not entirely so. The four of you will never forget each other. The bonds of the twins are too strong to be severed so easily. And there is a hidden door within my garden that connects to a secret way behind Avallach's stable. Family is family, after all.

"Now, my dear," he said, turning to Aisling. "I think it would be best to get you out of this filthy rag and tend those wounds of yours." A shadow crossed his face. "I well remember what will lie beneath that dress. Caoimhe, would you be so kind? There should be something of Laoise's still in the cedar chest in her old chamber." He pointed to a door. "I will have the maid bring hot water and linens. If you would wash her back and bind the wounds, I would be eternally grateful."

"Of course," Caoimhe answered quietly. "Lean on my shoulder, Aisling," she offered, bending down to the other girl.

Aisling smiled up at her. "Thank you...sister."

When the young women had made their way slowly from the chamber, and he had sent the maid along with the promised items, Tadhg turned to Ailill and Fergal. "It will not be easy for either of you, you know."

The young men nodded.

"I have had occasion to dwell on both sides of the Fae fence, so I understand the problems all of you will face. It will be hard for Caoimhe, alone in Faerie, with even her own mother forgetting she existed. And for Aisling, unused to the ways of a wife. The two of you must ease their ways in their new worlds. You have the better time of it, to be sure.

"If ever you need anything, you come to me. Do not hesitate to call on me. My door is always open. I may be mortal now, but I believe I have a few good years left. Fergal—I would be honored if you will accept the gift of this house when I go on. That will keep the way safe until 'tis no longer needed."

"As you say, Magistrate," replied Fergal solemnly.

"Do not worry. I don't intend to relinquish it any time soon. And please, don't stand on formality, young one. You are marrying into my House." He raised an eyebrow in mock severity. "I *assume* you are marrying...?"

"Of course, Magis—Tadhg. I love Aisling with all my heart."

"And you, sprite—" Tadhg turned to Ailill. "I know the Fae hold no truck with formalities such as marriage, but Caoimhe is a good girl, who has been brought up a sheltered child. It would ease her heart to have a ceremony."

"If you think 'tis so, it is no balk to me."

"Good. Good." Tadhg lifted a kettle from the hearth and poured them each a mug of hot cider. "A toast—to the future. May it be as bright as your lover's eyes when she looks into your face."

Ailill and Fergal clanked mugs and drank to the toast.

* * *

The next morning, Tadhg sent messages to Seamus O'Connor and Ian and Kathleen Sinclair, inviting them to witness a double wedding.

Seamus was none too pleased at first to see Aisling and Fergal together, but when he saw what she had been willing to endure for the sake of his grandson, he kissed her carefully on each cheek. "The boy could do a grand sight worse," he murmured softly in her ear, and Aisling felt her cheeks grow hot.

"Thank you, Seamus," she acknowledged. "Your approval means a great deal to me."

Ian and Kathleen nodded politely to the young people, but Aisling was as familiar to them as their own daughter. They showed no sign of recognition.

"I am sorry, little one," Tadhg sighed in Caoimhe's ear, "'tis better so. Would you have them mourn you to the end of their days, not knowing where you have gone? This way, they will not regret what they do not know they've lost. At least they will be here to see the ceremony. Take what comfort there you can."

Caoimhe smiled sadly. "I appreciate your invitation to them, my Lord. It will make things easier to bear."

Both girls were dressed in borrowed finery from Laoise's trunk. Fergal had retrieved his own greatcoat, and Ailill wore one of Tadhg's, buttoned tight to hold his wings in check.

They were about to start the ceremony when they were interrupted by a soft knock on the rear door of the house. Tadhg excused himself and went to answer it. He returned with a slight woman wearing an iridescent shawl.

Aisling flew into Ailidh's arms with a muffled sob.

"There, there, love," soothed her mother. "I could

no' let both my babies marry and no' be present. Whatever road you may travel from here forward, you are still my child. Your father would no' come. I'm sorry. However, I have brought another guest.

"Tadhg—I hope you do no' mind. But what is a wedding without music?"

She gestured back down the hallway, and Avallach came forward, strumming Uaithne. The harp looked particularly sour to have to behave and pretend the Dagda was the musician of the two.

"I am most displeased you did not invite me yourself, brother," he murmured, wagging a finger at Tadhg, a twinkle in his eye, "when the twins are part of my own family...but I am here now anyway. Let the ceremony begin!"

Looking enormously pleased to have surprised the twins—and been surprised himself—Tadhg began the wedding.

Afterwards, Aisling could never remember much of the actual ceremony. It passed in a blur of shaken hands and boisterous laughter. She ate until she felt nigh to bursting but could never remember a single dish she had been served.

What she remembered most about the day was the Dagda sitting on the stair with a mug of ale playing the *geantrai* on Uaithne. Laughter and merriment spilled throughout the house and beyond its walls as neighbors heard the music and came to see what the fuss was all about. Then subtly, the music changed, and Avallach played in the autumn, letting the last of summer die so the world could continue on its way.

Long afterward, Aisling remembered being

introduced to one villager after another that day. Names and faces bombarded her until her head swam. But she was happy. They were to be her people now, and they were accepting her in spite of her slashed cheeks and her awkward ways. She did find a moment to sit quietly at the top of the stairs with her head resting in her mother's lap. She sighed contentedly as Ailidh stroked her hair.

"Are you happy, little one?"

"Oh, yes. Very much so."

"He seems a fine man, your Fergal. He will take good care of you."

"I know, Mother."

"Just remember the door in Tadhg's garden. If ever you need me, put a white rose on the top of the hedge, and I will meet you here or at Ailill's cottage."

"Do you think I did the right thing, Mother?"

"It isn't for me to say, lovey. Do *you* think you did the right thing?"

Aisling looked to the foot of the stairs, where Fergal stood laughing with Ailill and Caoimhe. He glanced up at her, and a smile lit his face like the summer sun bursting out of a cloudbank. He held up a hand to her.

"Oh, yes. I know I did."

"Then that is all that matters. Go on—go to him now. It is your wedding day."

Aisling kissed her mother's cheek and started down the stair.

She passed Ailill on his way up for his own quiet talk and smiled. "Are you satisfied now with what you learned of mortals?"

He glanced down the stairway to where his bride

stood with Fergal. "I suppose this is what comes of letting them see us," he replied, eyes dancing.

Aisling chuckled. "Last time I'll let you talk me into going to the Faire!"

She sobered as quickly as she had laughed. "I will miss you, Ailill. Do no' be a stranger." She hugged him hard.

"We are two halves of a whole, Aisling. I will never let you down," he promised returning the embrace, taking care for her back. "We're twins...don't ever forget."

"I won't."

"Now go on before your husband runs away with my wife!"

She laughed and went down to meet her husband.

Rie Sheridan Rose